What could be more ⌐
a walk in the clouds?

Cat turned back to get in line for the rope seat. But everyone else had already gone ahead, except for Aidan, who seemed, surprisingly, to be waiting for her.

"Thanks," Cat said, feeling her heart quicken just a touch.

The nature guide strapped Cat into the harness of the rope pulley, and when Amaranta gave the signal, Cat was lifted swiftly up through the cool mountain air. A walkway appeared through the swirling fog, suspended with ropes and winding through the treetops, and another set of pulleys deftly swung Cat onto it, with Aidan following right behind. After she'd regained her balance, Cat took in the scenery around her. Aside from the distant voices of the rest of the group echoing faintly every now and then, the cloud forest was peacefully quiet, and so beautiful. Heavy ferns dripping with dew hung from the trees, and flecks of brilliant color from orchids growing out of tree trunks spotted the milky-green horizon.

"Wow," Cat whispered. A sudden rustle in the branches above her made her jump, and she teetered on the edge of the walkway, nearly losing her balance.

A pair of warm hands caught her around the waist. "I've got you," Aidan said.

"Thanks," Cat stepped back, flustered. "I'm fine now."

Aidan dropped his hands quickly, shifting his gaze from her face to the trees....

Heart and Salsa

Suzanne Nelson

speak

An Imprint of Penguin Group (USA) Inc.

For Mom and Larry, with lots of love.
And for Christy, sister extraordinaire, in thanks for all the movie
marathons that got us through our growing pains.

SPEAK
Published by the Penguin Group
Penguin Group (USA) Inc.,
345 Hudson Street, New York, New York 10014, U.S.A.
Penguin Group (Canada), 90 Eglinton Avenue East, Suite 700, Toronto, Ontario, Canada M4P 2Y3
(a division of Pearson Penguin Canada Inc.)
Penguin Books Ltd, 80 Strand, London WC2R 0RL, England
Penguin Ireland, 25 St Stephen's Green, Dublin 2, Ireland
(a division of Penguin Books Ltd)
Penguin Group (Australia), 250 Camberwell Road, Camberwell, Victoria 3124, Australia
(a division of Pearson Australia Group Pty Ltd)
Penguin Books India Pvt Ltd, 11 Community Centre, Panchsheel Park,
New Delhi - 110 017, India
Penguin Group (NZ), Cnr Airborne and Rosedale Roads, Albany, Auckland 1310,
New Zealand (a division of Pearson New Zealand Ltd)
Penguin Books (South Africa) (Pty) Ltd, 24 Sturdee Avenue, Rosebank, Johannesburg 2196,
South Africa

Registered Offices: Penguin Books Ltd, 80 Strand, London WC2R 0RL, England

Published by Speak, an imprint of Penguin Group (USA) Inc., 2006

3 5 7 9 10 8 6 4

Copyright © Suzanne Nelson, 2006
All rights reserved
Interior art and design by Jeanine Henderson. Text set in Imago Book.

SPEAK ISBN 978-0-14-240647-2

Printed in the United States of America

Heart and Salsa

Monte Albán

Mercado de Abastos

Cat's Oaxaca

Basílica de Soledad

Museum of Contemporary Art

Cerro del Fortin

Auditorio Guelaguetza

Zócalo

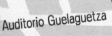

La Casa de Juarez

Utel Chocolate Posada
on Fco. Javier Mina

Application for the Students Across the Seven Seas
Study Abroad Program

Name: Caitlin Wilcox
Age: 16
High School: North Harbor High
Hometown: Boston, Massachusetts
Preferred Study Abroad Destination: Oaxaca, Mexico

1. Why are you interested in traveling abroad next year?

Answer: I want to explore the origins of Mexican-Spanish language, and the best place to do that is Central America.

(Truth: My mom just got remarried to a man she barely knows, and now we're living two thousand miles away from my old hometown in Scottsdale, Arizona. My psyche (not to mention my social life) could be damaged forever! I need some serious rehabilitation time in crystal-clear Mexican waters.)

2. How will studying abroad further develop your talents and interests?

Answer: I plan to get a degree in bilingual studies in college, and being immersed in Mexican daily life will help me to achieve fluency in Spanish.

(Truth: I plan to spend the summer beaching it with my BFF, Sabrina, which beats the heck out of "bonding" with stepdad Ted.)

3. Describe your extracurricular activities.

Answer: Former Member of the Scottsdale High Diving Team; Winner of the 2005 Arizona Diving Championship

(Truth: Every day I go to my new school (which I hate), sit alone at lunch (which I hate), walk home through a blinding snowstorm (which I hate), and spend the night waiting for my 8 P.M. IM session with Sabrina [the highlight of my sorry existence].)

4. Is there anything else you feel we should know about you?

Answer: I will use my athletic abilities and love of the outdoors to contribute as much as possible to the semester community service project.

(Truth: I'll do anything—ANYTHING—to get out of Boston for the summer! Do you hear me?!?)

Chapter One

When Caitlin Wilcox stepped off the plane at the Oaxaca airport, a wide smile spread across her face. The bright blue sky was dotted with a few marshmallowy clouds, and the midafternoon sun lit up the lush hillsides surrounding the small airport with an effervescent green. She had gotten on the plane in an overcast, drizzly Boston, and gotten off in a tropical Mexican paradise. She had two months of freedom ahead of her in this postcard-perfect place! Even when she saw a donkey, standing happily on the dirt runway, watching passengers deboard the puddle jumper, she laughed with

delight. The donkey was the first real sign that she was in a foreign country, and it sank in that she was finally here. It couldn't get much better than this.

But it could. Because just then she spotted Sabrina, her truest, dearest, best friend of years and years waving maniacally from the airport doorway. Cat grinned and waved back excitedly, but then froze when she saw that, standing next to Sabrina, holding her hand, was…a boy. Wait a minute…*a boy*? Cat blinked in surprise. But then she recognized the telltale glow in Sabrina's smile, and the sidelong glances of adoration she was casting at the tall, muscular, copper-haired hottie beside her. She'd seen that look on Sabrina's face too many times to keep track.

Cat shook her head, laughing. True, she hadn't expected this so soon into their summer, but this was so typically Sabrina. She'd probably met the guy on the plane, or maybe even in the terminal once she landed. It never took her long to find a new crush. She went through boys like they were chewing gum—five minutes and the flavor was gone. Cat had always felt sorry for the poor guys who fell hard for Sabrina and were devastated when she broke it off. This guy, cute as he was, was in for the same heartbreak, Cat was sure. It was just a matter of time. In all likelihood, Sabrina would be over him by the third date, and then she and Cat could get this summer started for real.

In every one of their nightly IM sessions and the dozens

of e-mails and phone calls they'd swapped since Cat had moved from Scottsdale, Arizona, to Boston, all she and Sabrina had talked about was making this trip together for the summer study abroad program. It was *supposed* to be a summer of girl bonding. A summer for Cat to forget how the rest of her old friendships had been lost with her move, the e-mails and calls from her diving team buds and class-mates petering off into a pathetic dribble.

Sabrina's was the only friendship that had survived, and as long as Cat had Sabrina to talk to, her old life in Scottsdale wasn't gone forever. This summer, Sabrina had promised to get Cat up to speed on everything she'd missed in Scottsdale, and Cat had vowed to perfect her Spanish, a language she loved. That was why she had wanted to come to Mexico. That, and her desperate desire to escape her new family and her new home.

As if her mom's whirlwind romance with Ted Starling hadn't been bad enough, she had to go and marry the guy! After dating for only three months! Cat had hoped she would've been more cautious after one failed marriage, but there was no accounting for adults…especially those on the rebound from a messy divorce. And to torture her even more, two months into the spring semester in Scottsdale, her mom and Ted forced her to say good-bye to her high school, her friends, and her home of sixteen years to move to a northeastern metropolis she'd never

even visited before. Faced with the possibility of spending a miserable summer in Boston, Cat had, with Sabrina's help, developed a master plan for escape.

But a boy had never been included in their master plan. Still, here he was, so Cat would make the best of it. Sabrina might go through boys at the speed of light, but she'd never forgotten about Cat in the process, so Cat would just deal. Besides, he wouldn't last long anyway.

Cat shifted her carry-on onto her shoulder and walked toward Sabrina and her new man.

"KitCat!" Sabrina waved, jumping up and down in her classic hyperdrive fashion from the other side of the tarmac. "Cat! Over here!"

"Easy, sweets," Cat heard the boy say to Sabrina. "I think she sees you. You've gotten the attention of the whole airport."

Sabrina ran to Cat, almost knocking her over with a hug.

"¡Hola, mi amiga!" she cried. *"Bienvenida a Mexico!* Omigod, it's so great to see you!" She held Cat at arm's length, looking her over.

Cat noticed Sabrina looked like her eco-friendly self as usual, her long legs set off in a dye-free hemp skirt. From the linen scarf she'd tied in her hair to her sage-green espadrilles, she looked like she was ready to take on the jungle in style.

"Where have the parentals been keeping you in Boston?" Sabrina said. "A dungeon? What happened to your tan?"

"It disappeared as soon as I left Arizona," Cat said, laughing. "Now I live in a state where the sun never shines. It's tough to tan in nonstop rain and snow."

Sabrina laughed, then motioned to her guy-of-the-hour, who easily slipped his arm around her waist. She beamed, giving him a peck on the cheek.

"Cat," she said, her voice rising with excitement, "this is Brian...my boyfriend."

Boyfriend!?! Cat barely managed to keep her jaw from dropping. When had this happened? Sabrina didn't give any guy *that* title. She always used safer, noncommittal words like "crush" or "date" or even just plain "friend." Still, even if he was Sabrina's "boyfriend," they couldn't have been dating for more than—what?—a nanosecond? Otherwise, Sabrina would have told her about him already in one of their daily chat sessions. They must have met recently, and Sabrina just hadn't had a chance to tell her yet in all the chaos of getting ready for this summer. That had to be the explanation. And what did Cat care anyway? In two or three days, Brian would be history.

Cat smiled, already feeling a touch of sympathy for him at the thought of his soon-to-be ex-boyfriend status. "Nice to meet you, Brian," she said. "I've..." Her voice died. She'd been about to say, "I've heard so much about you," until she realized she hadn't.

Luckily, Brian jumped right in with, "Nice to meet you, too." He smiled, showing gleaming white, perfectly straight

teeth worthy of any J. Crew ad. "Sabrina never told me her best friend was so good-looking."

Sabrina playfully slapped his arm. "Don't get any ideas, Bri. You're all mine."

Cat laughed politely while she fought a battle with her eyes to keep them from rolling. Well, Sabrina'd picked a charmer this time. Cat didn't know how the compliment could have come across as any less genuine. Unlike Sabrina, who always looked like she had stepped out of an environmentally friendly fashion magazine, Cat kept her blond hair in a no-mess, no-fuss pixie cut, and she favored a comfy cotton cami and lounge pants over skirts and heels any day. Her guy friends in Scottsdale had always seen her as the low-maintenance type, never afraid to break a nail or get a little dirty—perfect to play flag football with, but not to date. Not the kind of girl guys pegged as pretty right away, especially guys like Brian. But, to give him the benefit of the doubt, this was probably an awkward moment for him, too.

As Cat watched the two of them, Brian leaned over and nuzzled Sabrina's neck, making her giggle. Okay, so maybe he wasn't feeling quite as awkward as Cat was, after all.

"Well, ladies," he said, sliding Cat's carry-on off her shoulder and onto his own, where he already had his and Sabrina's. "Should we see about the rest of our luggage?"

"Sounds good," Cat said. But as Brian walked ahead of

them, she gave Sabrina a wink. It was their long-practiced signal for an emergency one-on-one chat session.

Sabrina read it immediately and grabbed Brian's arm. "Bri, could you keep an eye out for Cat's stuff?" she asked him. "It's a Scottsdale Diving Club duffel bag…you can't miss it. We're going to go find the restroom."

That made Cat happy. So Sabrina still remembered that she always packed her stuff in her favorite diving duffel. Back in Arizona, she'd used it to carry her suit, chamois, and other gear for diving meets. But since the move to Boston, the bag had been sitting unused, collecting dust in her closet, until she'd pulled it out for this trip.

"No prob," Brian said. "I'll meet you at the baggage claim. Then we can find the program bus."

Sabrina playfully latched onto Cat's arm, dragging her into the ladies' room, as Brian walked away. "I can't believe you're here!" she said. "I missed you so much."

"I missed you, too." Cat smiled. "So…when did this whole thing with Brian happen? You haven't even been here a full day, Sabrina! This might be a record, even for you." She slapped her lightly on the arm. "Was he on your plane or something? Details…now!"

Sabrina blushed. "Actually, it was before that…" She grinned sheepishly. "I was dying to tell you about him." She pulled a brush from her purse and ran it through her wavy auburn hair. "But it all happened so fast, and then I didn't know how to tell you over the phone."

"Wait…How long have you been dating?" Cat asked, suddenly feeling like maybe she had missed out on a little more than she'd thought.

"We met a couple of weeks after you moved," Sabrina said hesitantly.

"Three whole months ago?" Cat cried. So she'd missed out on everything, then.

"I know I should've told you," Sabrina said. "But you're not mad, are you?" Worry flickered across her face. "You sounded so down in Boston, and I didn't want to make you feel worse. And then I thought I'd surprise you when you got here! Isn't he great?"

Cat let out a small sigh, but even as she did she could not help smiling at Sabrina's giddy grin. She knew how to play this role by heart. "He does seem nice," she managed. It was kind of an unspoken rule between them: when Sabrina was crushing on a guy, it was Cat's job to humor her, and when Cat was dealing with family crapola, it was Sabrina's job to help her forget about it. "Is he more *Pretty in Pink*, *Sixteen Candles*, or *Some Kind of Wonderful*?"

"Well," Sabrina giggled. "He looks a little like Eric Stoltz in *Some Kind of Wonderful*, don't you think? But he's way more like Jake in *Sixteen Candles*."

"I always thought Jake was your type," Cat teased.

Ever since they first met, bunking in the same cabin at summer camp back in fifth grade, she and Sabrina had shared a love, and sometimes total obsession, for the

8

movies John Hughes had directed in the 1980s. Sabrina had smuggled her older sister's videos of *The Breakfast Club* and *Sixteen Candles* into camp for a midnight movie marathon, and she and Cat had kept up the tradition by having a John Hughes marathon after their midterms and finals each year after that. This was the first year they'd broken the tradition.

"So," Cat said, "how did you and Brian meet?"

Sabrina dabbed on her Nature's Kiss lip gloss (the only kind she ever used...totally organic). "We met at the Tri-valley student government convention. He's the student-body president at Cougar Canyon High."

"You're dating the president of Scottsdale's rival school?" Cat said. Sabrina, who wanted to be a lawyer someday, had jumped right into school politics and community-service organizations in high school and had been elected class president at Scottsdale High. "Isn't there a school code forbidding romance across enemy lines?"

"You forget I help make the codes." Sabrina giggled. "Anyway, on one of our first dates, I mentioned Helping Hands EDU and how you and I were going through the S.A.S.S. program this summer. When I told him about the hands-on conservation studies and community service, Bri got hyped and applied through Cougar Canyon. He's thinking of going the prelaw track in college next year, and he says he wants to get in as much community service as he can. We just have so much in common!" She smiled.

"And, Cat, I've never felt this way about a guy before. You know how I normally get."

"What, you mean breaking the heart of nearly every datable guy in Scottsdale?" Cat laughed. "Don't remind me. I'm the one who wiped away their tears, remember?"

"Come on, I'm not that bad," Sabrina said with mock hurt. "I just like to have fun, and those guys got too serious too fast. This time, with Bri, it's different."

"Uh-huh," Cat said. "I'll believe it when I see it."

"No, really," Sabrina said seriously. "I think I'm in love with him."

Cat studied Sabrina's sober face. This *was* different. Sabrina had never used the word "love" with any guys in the past. She'd always said that she wanted to save it for someone really special, and now she was uttering the word with complete sincerity.

"Wow," Cat said. "That's big news, Sabrina. Congrats."

Sabrina giggled. "And I haven't even told you what a fantastic kisser he is yet."

"Better than Bobby Miller last semester?"

"Ugh, don't remind me of that traumatic experience." Sabrina grimaced. "There should be a law against tongue piercings."

"My guess is most piercings don't end in chipped teeth." Cat laughed. "It was a freak accident."

"Yeah, that cost my parents a couple hundred dollars in

dental bills," Sabrina said. "Remember the lie you came up with to explain what happened? My parents actually believed that I'd let you drag me onto the three-meter high dive to teach me that double-back-flip thingy. *And* that you'd managed to miraculously cure my fear of heights."

"Yeah, well, it was better than having to tell them you broke curfew, snuck out your window, and headed to Research Park for a midnight make-out session with Bobby," Cat said, laughing. "If I hadn't covered for you that night, you'd probably be grounded 'til college, at least. And then you'd have no more dates *to* break curfew with."

"Shh." Sabrina giggled. "It's bad luck to even say things like that out loud. And *you* could definitely benefit from a little wild-child behavior yourself."

"I'm not here five minutes and you're already trying to fix my social life." Cat laughed. "It's like not a day has passed since Scottsdale." She'd always been less of a socialite than Sabrina, enjoying spending one-on-one time with her over the parties Sabrina begged her to come along to. She was a sun baby instead, loving anything and everything outdoors, especially the Olympic-size swimming pool at the Scottsdale Diving Club where, in her former happy life, she'd spent hour after hour practicing her diving. But Cat had learned to enjoy the occasional party as well as the art of makeup application from Sabrina, and Sabrina had learned to water-ski and in-line skate from

Cat—things neither of them would ever have tried on their own. For all their differences, they'd always been each other's system of checks and balances.

"We are going to have an amazing summer!" Sabrina gave Cat another hug as they made their way out of the bathroom and toward the baggage claim. "Just think...this is our first chance to make a difference helping people *and* raise our environmental consciousness."

"Recycling just doesn't do it for you, huh?" Cat laughed. She'd never forget the half-hour lecture she'd brought on by throwing a soda can into the trash in front of Sabrina. Sabrina was an overachiever, sure, but it was because she was passionate about changing the world. She wasn't just accumulating massive amounts of community-service activities to bulk up her résumé. Nope...she actually believed she could achieve world peace, heal the holes in the ozone, *and* save the rain forests all in the next decade.

"Don't get me wrong. This summer won't be all work and no play." She grinned. "Beaches, siestas, fiestas, a boyfriend for me"—she winked—"and maybe one for you, too?"

"No pressuring me, now." Cat smiled, elbowing Sabrina. "I'm suffering from postdivorce dating stress syndrome anyway. I have no desire to lay my heart out on the table so that some seemingly nice guy can come along and dissect it...piece by piece. You saw what happened to my mom. My dad cared more about his job than her. Why should I set myself up to get hurt like that when I'm perfectly happy on my own?"

"The divorce was two years ago, Cat," Sabrina said.

"Yeah, but the trauma could last a lifetime," Cat countered, to which Sabrina just laughed and rolled her eyes. Sabrina knew more about the divorce than the rest of Cat's friends. It was Sabrina who had cheered alongside Cat's mom at all of Cat's diving meets when her dad was away traveling. It was Sabrina who had spirited Cat out of her house when Cat's parents were fighting. Cat's dad was never home much, since he traveled about eight or nine months of the year for his international business consultant job. When he *was* home, he and her mom fought about his *never* being there. Her mom wanted a full-time husband, but her dad had other ideas, not ever ready (or willing) to cut back on his job or travel. Finally, he decided to stop coming home at all between trips.

While part of Cat was relieved when her dad filed for the divorce, another part was devastated, and furious, to see him moving out permanently. In the months after the divorce, whenever Cat showed up at Sabrina's house after school in tears, Sabrina dropped everything to listen. Sabrina's mom always kept Cat's favorite Trader Joe's cheesecake stocked in their fridge as emergency comfort food, and the girls knew how to put it to good use. Cat

would vent between platefuls, and before she knew it, she'd be feeling better. She'd always have Sabrina to thank for that.

Sabrina's sagas with guys proved a great distraction for Cat during the divorce, too. Sabrina would ramble on and on about her latest crush, recounting a horrific date she'd had, or how her mom had caught her making out on the couch, and soon enough, Cat would be smiling again. When she was at Sabrina's house, she was in a world filled with such normal problems—crushes, dates from hell, clothing crises. She'd liked being Sabrina's confidante about boys back then. And she could do it now, too, for as long as this latest crush of hers lasted (she was thinking breakup by next Friday, tops).

"At least I don't have to listen to my parents' fights anymore," Cat admitted to Sabrina. "But now I have to deal with my mom's current delirium instead. I don't believe this whole love-at-first-sight song and dance she's been giving me about Ted."

"Whoa, someone's been listening to a little too much 'Rage Against the Machine' lately, hasn't she?" Sabrina laughed. "I'm telling you, that music's going to make you a cynic forever. It's time to give the iPod a rest."

"Never. I wouldn't survive the withdrawal." Cat laughed.

"You need a diversion, or you're in danger of becoming a complete love-a-phobic." Sabrina grinned, and Cat could practically see her matchmaking wheels turning. "You know what the perfect remedy is? A full-on, spontaneous make-out session. Yup. And I guarantee there's going to be some hot guys in our program this summer you won't be able to resist."

"Sorry, not happening," Cat said. "Boyfriends are seriously overrated."

"Look, just because your parents got divorced doesn't mean all relationships end badly," Sabrina said. "Not every guy is a workaholic like your dad is. And speaking of the Amazing Disappearing Man, have you talked to him lately?"

"Oh, we've talked," Cat said. "We just never say much of anything important to each other." She'd only recently started to make a real effort to talk to her dad again. He was the one who'd pushed for the divorce and left her mom and her, and she hadn't quite gotten over that yet. "He called me a couple days ago, from New Zealand. Or at least I think he said New Zealand." Cat sighed. "He travels so much, I can't keep track of where he is."

"At least you're on speaking terms again," Sabrina said. "That's something. And now your mom's totally happy with her new hubby, right?"

"Delirious is more like it," Cat said flatly. "If I'd had to watch them be all lovey-dovey for one more day, I was going to call child protective services. It's abuse." She grimaced. "And I still can't believe Ted accepted that tenure position at North Harbor U and made us move. Who cares if their history department is *'magnifique'* or whatever he

called it? And he's the cause of my mom's plunge into insanity, too. I mean, what kind of mother marries a guy she barely knows! He could be a serial killer. This is the type of stuff *they're* supposed to lecture *us* about!"

"Somehow, I doubt that Ted's a serial killer." Sabrina giggled.

"Probably not, but he is weird," Cat said. "He's home every night, and that alone thrills my mom. But he doesn't say much. Mom says he's a deep thinker, not a big talker." She shrugged. "Oh, and I've discovered another freakish thing about him. When we went out for breakfast last week, he cut his doughnuts into pieces and ate them with a knife and fork. Mom says he doesn't like getting sugar glaze all over his fingers."

"I don't blame him," Sabrina said. "I wouldn't touch a doughnut either. Do you know how many toxins are in fried food like that?" She giggled. "Okay, so maybe Ted's a bit weird. But he's nice, with a little touch of metrosexual thrown in for good measure. I'd like to see him shop. I bet the man's got great taste."

"Come to think of it," Cat said, "Mom teases him some-times about how much time he spends in the bathroom fixing his hair, and he loves Banana Republic."

The two of them looked at each other and burst out laughing, and suddenly Cat felt like only a day had passed since she last saw Sabrina, instead of months. She and Sabrina could still laugh together, just like they used to.

And even with Brian in the picture, Cat had a feeling that this summer would be the cure for her Boston blues. She was thousands of miles away from that city and from Ted, and just the thought of not having to face either one of them for a whole two months was enough to keep her smiling.

Once Cat and Sabrina found Brian at the baggage claim, it only took a few minutes with customs officials before they made their way outside. The blue-and-yellow Helping Hands bus was easy to spot, especially since there was only a handful of cars scattered around the airport parking lot. A middle-aged man with a chestnut beard, wearing a brown fedora hat and cargo pants, stood next to the bus, waving them over.

"Buenos tardes," he said, shaking hands with each of them. *"Me llamo* Sebastian. I'm the program coordinator for Helping Hands. Welcome to Mexico." He put their suitcases under the bus and handed each of them a yellow canvas bag.

"Inside, there's an Oaxaca city guide, a study guide, a semester agenda, and a Helping Hands T-shirt," Sebastian said. "We're waiting for one more flight to arrive, so please take a seat on the bus. Once we have the other students, we'll leave for Oaxaca."

Cat followed Sabrina and Brian onto the bus, which was nearly full with students. Brian quickly sat down in the only

open two-seater left, grabbed Sabrina by the waist, and pulled her down next to him. She squealed and laughed, then kissed him. Cat looked for a seat nearby, but the only ones remaining were at the other end of the bus.

"There're a few seats in the back," Cat said. "We could look for something together…"

Her voice died away. Nothing she'd said had registered with the two lovebirds, who were now head-to-head in a snuggle fest. Normally, *Sabrina* would have been the one to search out three seats together. Normally, she didn't even like spending too much one-on-one time with a crush, because it made guys "too dependent" on her. But, in this case, Cat realized, Sabrina wasn't acting entirely like her normal self.

Cat shrugged and made her way down the aisle to the first open seat, which was already half occupied by a guy. She could see only the top of his brown-haired head, which was bent intently over a book.

"Excuse me," Cat said. "Is this seat taken?"

His head lifted, and a pair of deep emerald eyes in a tan face looked up at her. "It's all yours." He gave her a friendly smile. "I'm Aidan."

"Cat," she said, sitting down. "Thanks for the seat."

"No problem." He nodded, then reopened his book, becoming totally absorbed in it again within seconds.

A few minutes later, Sebastian climbed on board with

the last of the students, and the bus pulled away from the curb just as a high-pitched giggle sounded from the direction of Sabrina's seat. Cat reached into her small carry-on and pulled out her journal, which in a dark moment two years ago she'd named Diary of My Dysfunctional Life. The smarmy family counselor her mom had forced her to talk to while the divorce was being finalized had given it to her, telling her to "give it a name that would make it personal— like an old friend." After four sessions filled with uncooperative silence, Cat finally convinced her mom that there was no way she was spilling her guts to a Dr. Phil Wannabe. She and the counselor parted ways, but the journal survived the breakup. Since the move to Boston, she'd been filling up the pages faster than ever. She opened it and read the final lines from yesterday's entry: "I can't wait to see Sabrina in Mexico. We're going to have the best summer ever!"

She shook her head as she remembered how it was Sabrina who had come up with the idea for Cat's summer jailbreak back in March. Instead of logging on at eight P.M. for their nightly IM session, Sabrina had been so excited that she'd called Cat instead. She'd gushed about the Helping Hands program and how she was applying through S.A.S.S.

"Come with me!" Sabrina said. "We could spend every day together, and I could fill you in on the latest Scottsdale

gossip. Plus, you'd get to swim in the ocean again, and by the time the semester was over, you'd be fluent in Spanish! You're the only person I know who actually enjoyed mandatory Spanish with old Señora Doring the Boring. This program was made for you. I e-mailed you the link to the online brochure. Check it out."

As Cat looked through the brochure later that night, she realized it was true. It was like the Helping Hands program had been designed with her in mind. She stared longingly at the photos of students snorkeling in a clear ocean with sea turtles and tropical fish, and dreamed of what it would feel like to be in that water.

In Arizona, she'd been in the Scottsdale Diving Club and had made it onto the varsity Scottsdale High team. She could never get enough of the water. Her mom used to tease that she had a mermaid for a daughter, but it had been a long time since she'd called her that. If she went to Mexico, though, that amazing ocean would be hers for the swimming.

Still, it was pointless to dream about a trip she could never take. Her mom had already informed her that this summer was going to be a "bonding time" for her and Ted. She'd never let Cat ditch all that family fun for Mexico. Cat was condemned to suffer the summer from hell, so she closed the Internet link, her heart sinking as the photos of tropical paradise vanished.

But after just a few horrid weeks in Boston, struggling

through lonely lunches in her school caf, she knew beyond a doubt that there was no way she would survive a summer in the city. Feeling like she had nothing to lose, she appealed to her mom and Ted to let her go to Mexico. And—shocker—they'd caved almost immediately. It might have had something to do with the fact that, since the move, her usually good grades had taken a plunge. Or the fact that every time her mom asked her, "Why don't you invite some of your new friends over to the house this weekend?" Cat replied drily with, "What new friends?" But Cat guessed it was probably her refusal to join the North Harbor Diving Club and varsity team that had really freaked them out enough to let her go.

In Arizona, diving had been everything to her. She'd won the state championship last year with her reverse two-and-a-half somersault with a tuck, but in Boston the last thing she felt like doing was diving. Still, her mom and Ted had insisted on having Coach Landon, the coach at the North Harbor Diving Club, give them a tour of the state-of-the-art indoor diving center.

"Your reputation on the junior national diving circuit preceded you," Coach Landon told Cat as he shook her hand. "I've heard great things. Our regional diving organization is a little short staffed at the moment, so I coach the club team and North Harbor High varsity team. The practices for the high school meets are held here as well. We'd be glad to have you on both teams."

"Thanks, but I'm not interested," Cat said matter-of-factly.

"Well, you don't have to decide right now," the coach said. "Take some time to think it over. Look around at the pool area for as long as you like."

"Isn't he great?" her mom said overeagerly after he left them alone, looking expectantly at Cat for the slightest sign of enthusiasm.

"North Harbor has the best regional diving club around," Ted said, "and you could meet some kids at school through varsity. With the indoor pool, you can even dive in a blizzard." He was giving her the old teacher-to-student pep talk. That was the one thing Cat had noticed about him. Sometimes when he was trying too hard to please her, he shifted into professor mode.

The heated pool with its pristine water had looked inviting, and for one minute Cat could almost feel her toes teetering on the edge of the five-meter platform, flexed for a dive. But then the thrill of imagining it died away. Here, she wouldn't have Nikki, Sam, and Jason, her Scottsdale Diving Club teammates, cheering her on. Here, she'd be diving with strangers under fluorescent lights instead of the clear blue Arizona sky. Where was the fun in that?

"Forget it," she said. "I don't care about diving anymore."

"Cat, honey," her mom said, "maybe just give it a try, and then we'll see—"

"What's the point?" Cat said. "Next year, after I graduate, I'm going back to Arizona U anyway."

"A lot could happen between now and then, kiddo," Ted
said. "You might change your mind, make new friends—"

"Why bother?" Cat said flatly. "It'll never be the same."
She'd left the pool area without looking back, and that was
the last time she'd heard mention of diving from them.

So she'd sworn off diving, her friendships in Scottsdale
were fading because of the whole long-distance thing,
and her friendship prospects in Boston were looking
bleak, too. Sabrina was the only friend from Arizona who
had kept IMing and calling diligently through it all, and the
only thing that had made sense to Cat was to spend this
last summer with her before starting their senior years
apart.

Now, though, after she'd begged her mom and Ted to
let her go, things weren't happening the way she'd imagined. Not with Brian's unexpected appearance. Cat closed
the journal and slipped it back into her bag. So she'd just
have to readjust her mind-set about this summer. No big-
gie. She sighed, louder than she'd planned, making Aidan
look up from his book.

"Homesick already?" he asked.

"Ha!" The hard laugh popped out of her before she
could stop it. "I mean, no, not at all," she corrected with a
smile. "Just thinking."

"In my experience, thinking doesn't usually cause sighs

like that unless it's thinking about homework, family stuff, or a *really* bad breakup. And since we don't have any homework yet, I'm guessing it's one of the other two?"

Cat thought about that before answering. "It's *definitely* not over a guy. It's more family and friend stuff. But nothing a few days here won't fix, I hope."

"Well, I'm relieved about the guy part." Aidan grinned. "I might get a little nervous sitting next to you if you were plotting revenge against the entire male sex."

"Don't worry," Cat said. "You're safe with me. I don't have anything against guys as friends. Believe me, I've befriended quite a few who plotted revenge against us *girls.*" She laughed. "Not against me, specifically," she added at Aidan's look of mock panic. "Against my best friend. She might hold the record for the largest number of breakups in a single year. That's her giggling up there."

"Oh, so *that's* the friend part of the sighing," he said.

Cat nodded. "Friend-with-surprise-new-boyfriend part."

"Enough said." Aidan smiled. "But now that it's out of your system, no more sighing, okay? It's just not right in a setting like this." He pointed out the window, and Cat glanced up and gasped. The airport was long gone, replaced with lush junglelike hillsides silhouetted against the bright blue, cloudless sky.

"It's beautiful," Cat said just as someone in the seat behind them started humming loudly.

"The Sierra Madre del Sur," Aidan said, holding up his

book, which looked like a nature guide to Oaxaca. "I'm reading up on the landscape."

The humming behind them got louder, and suddenly a voice broke into song.

"Blue Spanish eyes, prettiest eyes in all of Mexico.

True Spanish eyes, please smile for me once before I go.

Soon, I'll return, bringing you all the love your heart can hold…"

Aidan laughed. "Pete, could you give it a rest?" he called over his shoulder. "You're scaring my seatmate."

A grinning, boyish-looking face with big, wire-framed glasses appeared over the seat, followed by a girl's face with uncannily similar eyes and the same-color blond hair.

"I told him to shut up," the girl said, elbowing Pete. "If he sings that song one more time, he won't live to see Oaxaca."

"I'm just singing about the future love of my life," Pete said. "She's waiting for me…naked on a Mexican beach somewhere."

"A very disturbing picture." The girl grimaced. "Why am I cursed with a hormonally challenged twin brother?"

"Mock me now," Pete said to his sister and Aidan. "But I will find her. I can feel it." He studied Cat, then said with a melodramatic bow of his head, "In the meantime, Don Juan, king of romance and seduction, at your service."

Cat laughed at the absurdness of this scrawny guy seducing anyone. If the words had been spoken by a different

type of guy, like, say, Brian, they would have come across as slimy. But from Pete, they were just plain funny.

Aidan nodded toward them. "Cat, meet Pete and Rachel Sims. We all go to the same school in Manhattan."

"Don't let Pete throw you," Rachel said. "I blame it on the fact that he was born second. Possible oxygen deprivation. Aidan and I are perfectly normal, really."

Cat laughed. "I guess I'll have to trust you on that one."

Just then, the bus speakers clicked on, and Cat glanced up to see Sebastian standing in the aisle holding a microphone.

"Buenas tardes," he said, "and welcome to the Helping Hands EDU study abroad program. This will be one of the only times I will be addressing you in English." He smiled. "Since it's your first day with us, I'll go easy on you. But as of tomorrow morning, I will be speaking only Spanish, and you will do the same. Since there are no classes in the traditional sense of the word, speaking Spanish when you interact within the program setting will be part of your foreign-language education. All of you have taken at least midlevel Spanish, but our goal is to have you speaking fluently by the time you leave here in August."

"All the better to woo my Spanish lady with," Pete whispered dreamily.

"Is he usually like this?" Cat whispered to Aidan.

"Always," Aidan said with a laugh. "I've got to hand it to him, though. The guy's an eternal optimist."

"Spanish isn't the only language you'll be hearing in Oaxaca," Sebastian continued. "Oaxaca is one of the only truly authentic colonial cities left in Mexico, but it also has a large population of Mexican Indians from precolonial days. The tribes here speak different dialects, including Nuhuatl, Zapotec, Mixtec, and even Mayan. But nearly everyone speaks Spanish as well, so you should get along just fine." He scanned the students' faces. "For our semester community-service project, we'll be building a school for orphaned children living in Oaxaca. The school will provide an education for children while they're awaiting placement with families. Because of limited vacant land near the orphanage, the building site is within driving distance at the edge of town. You'll be working there Mondays through Fridays from six A.M. to one P.M, beginning tomorrow. This schedule will help us avoid working during the hottest part of the day. A bus will pick you up in the town square, take you to the site, and bring you back. Afternoons are reserved for you to explore Oaxaca or to work on your schoolwork."

A few students snickered quietly at the mention of schoolwork, making Sebastian smile.

"Yes, for you skeptics out there laughing, there will be some schoolwork. We don't have a by-the-book classroom structure, but our program offers eco-education instead— studies on Mexican culture, history, archaeology, and environmental conservation. The study guide you received has

ample space for taking notes, and there's also an overview of important Mexican historical, cultural, and environmental facts inside. Several teachers from the Universidad de Oaxaca, as well as some of the host parents who have expertise in these areas, will be guest lecturers during our organized field trips. You'll visit the ancient Mayan ruins surrounding Oaxaca, turtle-nesting sights at the Centro Mexicano de la Tortuga, and the coffee plantations and tribal villages surrounding the city. There will also be a snorkeling expedition and a trip to Mexico City.

When she heard Sebastian mention snorkeling, Cat envisioned warm, sparkling blue waters. The last time she'd swum in the ocean was on a trip to San Diego with her parents when she was five, back when her dad had been home more than just a few months out of the year. She'd played in the waves for hours, until her lips turned blue from the cold and her mom dragged her kicking and screaming to a warm towel on the beach. It would be heaven to swim for hours in the ocean again, diving beneath the waves to watch the fish float by.

Sebastian continued, "After each field trip, you will write a three-to-five-page report, in Spanish, on a historic, cultural, or scientific aspect of what you experienced. There will also be a comprehensive midterm and final exam covering the sights we've seen along with an oral Spanish exam to test your language skills."

"That means leave your exotic-girl fantasy world out of it, Pete," Cat heard Rachel mutter behind her.

Cat grinned as Sebastian finished his lecture. Even without Sabrina to talk to, this bus ride to Oaxaca was entertaining. Aidan, Pete, and Rachel seemed nice, and getting to know them might not be a bad idea, especially if Sabrina was going to be oogling Brian for the next couple days. Cat snuck a sidelong glance at Aidan, who was intently focused on his book again. He *was* cute.

But she quickly shook that thought off. She wasn't going down that road...nuh-uh. Liking a guy was asking for trouble. It was always better, and safer, to keep guys as friends. No guy had ever looked at her as potential dating material anyway. In fact, Jason and Sam, her best boy buds in the Scottsdale Diving Club had always treated her like one of the guys. She could outdive both of them any day, and they'd thought that was cool. But sexy? Nope. And that was just fine by Cat, because she never, ever wanted to have her heart broken, not after she'd seen what her mom went through with her dad. Cat remembered all those nights hearing her mom's muffled crying from behind her bedroom door. Her mom might be happy for now, but love could be agony, that much she'd learned, and she certainly wasn't going to let it get in the way of her great summer plans.

Chapter Two

Cat knew the minute the town of Oaxaca came into view that this was a city she could love. It was spread out in the valley below the road, surrounded by thickly forested mountains. Brightly painted houses in red, blues, and yellows with red-tiled roofs dotted the city. Some areas resembled crowded shantytowns, while other areas were more spread out, with larger, stately villas and majestic churches.

The bus wound its way onto the narrow city streets, passing vibrant houses with decorative wrought iron laced over their windows, stray dogs lazily snoozing on porch steps, and barefoot children playing on sidewalks. Mexican women in flowered skirts were selling woven rugs, baskets, and fruits and vegetables in an outdoor market, and some were entering a church. Everywhere Cat looked, she saw color—in the flowers blooming, in the buildings, and in the clothing the townspeople were wearing.

When the bus stopped in front of a large, open square where people were milling around in the late-afternoon sunlight, Cat felt a rush of excitement. Here she was in a new country, far away from doughnut-cutting Ted and rainy Boston. Soon, she'd be surrounded by people speaking the most beautiful language in the world (in her opinion at least), and she'd have fresh air every day, a killer suntan, and, best of all, freedom.

"Your host families are joining us tonight for a welcome dinner here in the Plaza de Armas," Sebastian said, "better known as the *zócalo*—the heart of the city. It will give you a chance to get acquainted with them and sample some of our country's delicious food. Afterward, your host families will show you to their homes."

As Cat gathered her things, she saw Sabrina motioning to her that she'd meet her outside. Cat waved to Rachel and Pete, who were bickering over whose bag was whose, and then turned to Aidan.

"Thanks again for the seat," she said.

"No problem," Aidan said. "I'll see you later. And remember, no more sighing."

Cat smiled. "I'll try my best."

As soon as Cat stepped off the bus, Sabrina rushed over to her. "Can you believe this place?" she said, already snapping pictures with her camera. "I'm so glad your mom let you come. It wouldn't have been the same without you."

"Thanks," Cat said with a smile. "I'm glad I'm here, too."

"Listen," Sabrina said, casting one glance back at Brian, who was waiting a few feet away. "Even though Brian's along this summer, that doesn't mean you and I aren't going to have some serious girl bonding. I was thinking, tomorrow night after we're done with program stuff, we could go exploring."

"In other words, you want to take advantage of my skilled Spanish to help you get around the city," Cat teased.

"Of course." Sabrina smiled. "You know I barely scraped by in level-three Spanish this year, and you wouldn't leave me stranded with my Spanglish, would you?"

"That would be scary." Cat laughed. "Tomorrow sounds great. Then you can fill me in on the rest of the juicy dating details, too."

Sabrina giggled. "Don't I always?"

Once everyone had gathered their luggage, Sebastian led the way to the *zócalo*, a pretty square with a gazebo in its center surrounded by deep pink bougainvillea. Sidewalk cafés spilled from the archways of the surrounding buildings, and a huge, beautiful cathedral at one end of the square finished off the charming scene.

Sebastian stopped in front of a restaurant called La

Casa de la Abuelita, where a group of people was gathered in the outdoor seating area, all wearing name tags and smiling expectantly. He paired each student off with a host family, making introductions and then sending each newly acquainted group to sample the buffet. When it was Cat's turn, he led her to a middle-aged man with a weathered face and glasses standing arm and arm with a beautiful, full-figured woman with short, spiky raven hair. They both grinned eagerly as Cat approached. There was a girl with them, too, who was staring at Cat warily, wearing more of a frown than a grin. She looked close to Cat's age, with creamy coffee-colored skin; dark, shoulder-length hair; and velvety chocolate eyes.

"Cat, this is José and Abril Canul, your host parents," Sebastian said. "They own one of the best art galleries in Oaxaca. They have the widest collection from the Trique, Zapotec, and Mixtec tribes in this area. And José is a descendant of the ancient Maya."

"That's amazing," Cat said, shaking their hands. "I'd love to see the art gallery sometime."

"*Sí, sí,*" José said. "*Claro que sí.* Of course."

"And you're lucky to be living with one of our best program advisers, too—the Canuls' daughter, Itzel." Sebastian motioned to the still-guarded-looking girl.

"Each of our advisers brings a certain talent to the program," Sebastian explained, "and Itzel is our own resident revolutionary." He laughed. "She's so passionate about this

country, she may just end up running it someday." He looked past them to where other students were anxiously waiting to meet their hosts. "Well, I have more introductions to make, but I'll check on you later."

As he left, Cat reached out her hand to greet Itzel. "Nice to meet you, Itzel," she started with a smile.

But Itzel didn't return the smile or extend a hand. Instead she crossed her arms, forcing Cat to drop her own hand awkwardly. "If it's too hard for you to pronounce my name," she said slowly in English, enunciating each word a little too loudly, like Cat was a child, "just call me Izzie."

"It's not too hard," Cat said, taken aback. She hadn't mispronounced it before... had she? "I've taken Spanish in school."

Izzie smirked. "So did all the other ones, but they still managed to get it wrong."

"Other ones?" Cat asked blankly.

"The other American girls," Abril explained. "We've hosted students for the past three summers."

"You must enjoy it," Cat said, feeling slightly more at ease, despite Izzie's disconcerting stare. If the Helping Hands program had allowed the Canuls to host students for three years, they had to be doing something right. She turned to Itzel, hoping to reassure her. "I hate it when people mispronounce my name, too," she said. "And Caitlin isn't even hard. I'll make sure I get yours right."

But Izzie just replied with, "We'll see."

Abril smiled apologetically at Cat and turned toward Itzel, speaking to her in a waterfall of rapid, soft words. Cat tried to translate, but soon realized that whatever language they were speaking, though it held hints of Spanish, wasn't anything Cat had heard before. It was probably one of the other dialects Sebastian had mentioned earlier. She could tell by Abril's tone, though, that Itzel was getting a lecture. Oh, no. What if she'd gotten stuck with a host family who had a brat for a daughter? Izzie's behavior so far had been pretty standoffish. Weren't advisers supposed to be bubbling with enthusiasm? Or was that only the case in America?

Cat sighed. She didn't think she could deal with the surprise of Sabrina's new boyfriend *and* a mean host sister to boot. There was only so much a jet-lagged girl could take in one day.

Finally, Abril stopped talking, and Itzel looked up at Cat, attempting a smile, but Cat knew a forced one when she saw it.

Abril looked back and forth between Cat and Izzie, nodding in approval. Then she said to Cat, "*Tú y mi hijita llegaran a ser amigas pronto.* You and my daughter will become friends soon. Since you two will be sharing a room, you'll have lots of time to get to know each other."

"Sharing a room?" Cat repeated. She hadn't meant to sound surprised, but...*sharing a room?* Nothing in her program itinerary had mentioned that. Neither had Sebastian.

"Not everyone has the luxury of their own room here," Izzie said, stiffening. "*No es como los Estados Unidos.* It's not like the United States."

"No, no," Cat bumbled, flustered. "I didn't mean...I just wasn't expecting..."

Her voice died away. This was just great. Not ten minutes with her host family and she'd completely offended them. She didn't care that much about sharing a room. It had just caught her off guard. But how could she explain that to the Canuls?

"José and I will find a table," Abril offered, while José picked up Cat's duffel bag. "You must be hungry after your trip. Why don't you and Itzel get something to eat at the buffet? We'll join you in a few minutes."

Izzie smiled, a little too innocently, Cat thought, and led the way to the buffet.

"*¿Te gusta la comida Mexicana?*" Izzie asked, handing Cat a plate.

"Are you kidding?" Cat smiled. "Mexican food is my favorite."

"But this food is different from what Americans call 'Tex-Mex.'" Izzie pointed to the steaming platters of rich-smelling food. "Can I help you choose?"

Cat scanned the platters, looking for her favorite dish—cheese enchiladas. But the longer she looked, the less she recognized. "Um, sure," she agreed.

Izzie took Cat's plate and began filling it. "In Oaxaca,

mole sauce is our specialty. Here"—she dished up some meat covered in a dark brownish sauce onto Cat's plate—"is black mole with chicken made from chilies and chocolate." She stopped at the next platter. "Empanadas with pumpkin flowers." Down the buffet line Izzie went, putting samplings on Cat's plate, and deftly explaining each dish as she went. "Finally," Izzie said, pointing to a platter of small, dark nuggets giving off a tangy citrus aroma, "this is a favorite delicacy in our city. *Canasta de chapulines* in lime juice."

Cat tried to translate the words but drew a blank. "It smells delish." She took her plate from Izzie, with thanks, relieved that she'd had her to help with the food selection. Nothing in the buffet had looked anything like the chain Mexican food she'd had in the States.

After picking up gourd bowls filled with *tejate*, which Izzie explained was a Mexican "energy" drink made from corn, cocoa beans, cinnamon, and flowers, Cat and Izzie made their way back to the table. Izzie had sure been helpful. Cat hoped it was a sign that she'd decided that the newest American girl wasn't that bad, after all.

During the meal, Cat started to feel more comfortable and her Spanish started flowing more easily, too. She hoped she was starting to make up the ground she'd lost with her earlier faux pas about sharing a room. She could tell just from talking with them that the Canuls were kind people.

Abril and José talked excitedly about all the plans they had for the two girls over the summer. Abril wanted to teach Cat how to cook traditional Oaxacan food, and José invited her to come to their gallery as often as she liked.

"Oaxaca es la ciudad de mi corazón," José said. "The city of my heart. But there is much poverty here as well."

"That is why we have our gallery," Abril explained. "To help local tribes make money with their native crafts and artwork. *Y tus padres?* What do your parents do?"

"Oh," Cat said. "My father works as a consultant for a global computer engineering company." As soon as the words left her mouth, Cat saw Izzie give Abril a knowing look.

"Una princesa americana," Izzie muttered, barely audibly, to Abril, but then, at Abril's warning glare, quickly shut her mouth.

Cat saw Abril glance worriedly at her. Not wanting to get off on the wrong foot with Abril or José, she just took another bite of food, faking obliviousness. She'd understood Izzie perfectly, though. An American princess...that was what Izzie thought of her. It was almost funny how far from the truth that was.

"So you've probably traveled all over the world," Izzie said matter-of-factly.

"No," Cat said, getting really annoyed now. Why did Izzie seem so insistent on jumping to conclusions about her? With her, it was two steps forward, three steps *atrás.*

She glanced around at the other tables. There was Sabrina, chatting happily away with her host family, a young couple who already looked enchanted by her. Brian, at the table next to hers, was laughing with two teenage boys she could only assume were his host brothers. And Aidan was in the midst of an intense-looking conversation with an elderly, grandfather type. Everyone else seemed to be having a great time, and here she was, already struggling with her new roommate.

"Actually," Cat tried again, "my dad is the one who travels most of the time, not me. I don't see him much. My mother teaches elementary school, and my, um, stepfather is a university professor."

She still had trouble saying the word "stepfather," and it came out of her mouth awkwardly. The "step" part always made her think of the horrid stepparents portrayed in movies and books who locked kids in closets or kept them under the attic stairs. She barely knew Ted, but he didn't seem to fit that stereotype. And calling him "my other dad" or "my mom's new husband" sounded even freakier. This whole nonnuclear family lingo was definitely going to take some getting used to.

She was relieved when Izzie didn't push for any more info, and she focused on her food while Abril and José talked about the great things their city had to offer. Everything on her plate tasted fantastic, even though it was too dark in the square to see clearly what she was

eating. She had to judge by taste. The empanadas were a touch spicy, but the chicken with mole sauce was incredible. And the *chapulines* were a real treat, crunchy with a zingy lime coating.

"¿Te gustan?" Izzie asked with a smile. "You like them?"

"Sí," Cat said enthusiastically between bites, hoping to get on the right track with Izzie. *"Me gustan mucho."*

She'd already finished one helping and was enjoying a second when Sebastian stopped by their table.

"So," he said, "how is everything?"

"Great!" she said, trying to sound as cheery as possible.

"Perfecto." He looked down at her plate. "I'm impressed. Most of our students aren't brave enough to try *chapulines* on their first day in Mexico."

"Why not?" Cat asked.

"For many it's an acquired taste. After all, it's not every day people eat fried grasshoppers in the States."

Cat froze with another forkful of the insects just inches from her mouth. *Grasshoppers?!?* She had just eaten half a plateful of creepy crawlies? That's what *chapulines* meant! The advanced Spanish she'd taken in Scottsdale was fading away faster than she'd thought. And, just her luck, North Harbor High had offered only French and lower-level Spanish. She couldn't even enjoy her favorite subject in Boston, and it just figured that now she'd lost her Spanish skills on top of everything else.

She cast a quick glance at Izzie, who was hiding her

mouth with her napkin. From the way her shoulders were silently shaking, there was no question she was laughing. So, the whole thing had been a setup. Izzie was probably waiting for a squeamish scream to leave Cat's mouth, or worse, for Cat to run for the restroom. But Cat wasn't about to give her the satisfaction.

She straightened her shoulders and smiled. "Well," she said to Sebastian, "I think they're delicious." And with that, she calmly popped the last forkful of *chapulines* into her mouth. The look of surprise—and was there a hint of new-found respect?—on Izzie's face made them go down as easy as the sweetest cheesecake in the world.

By the time dinner ended and Cat left to go home with the Canuls, she could barely keep her eyes open. After getting up with the sun for her flight, then dealing with Sabrina's "guy surprise" and Izzie's princess-and-the-praying-man-tis test, she wanted nothing more than a comfy bed and good night's sleep. She tried to stifle a yawn as José unlocked the door of their Spanish colonial-style house, but Abril noticed right away.

"Estás muy cansada," she said, patting Cat's shoulder. "Itzel will show you to your bedroom now. Tomorrow, we'll give you a tour of the house. Itzel drives our car to the Helping Hands site every day, so you can go with her instead of taking the bus. She arrives early to help set up for the day's work."

"Gracias," Cat said, trying to keep smiling, despite her heavy eyelids.

"Buenas noches, Caitlin," Abril said. "Sleep well."

"Buenas noches." Cat nodded politely.

She guessed she was supposed to feel grateful that she didn't have to take the bus every day, but was she safe alone in a car with Izzie? First harmless fried grasshoppers, but what next? Mexican tarantulas in her shoes? If Izzie was a program adviser, weren't there rules about this kind of thing? Like, Thou shalt not torment the new American girl with plagues of locusts?

Izzie's disgruntled face as she led Cat down the narrow hallway assured Cat of one thing: tired or not, she wasn't going to sleep worry-free tonight. They walked in silence past a small kitchen, living room, and a set of double doors leading into a little courtyard at the center of the house. Cat could just make out a trickling fountain tucked in the shadows, and pot after pot of flowering plants.

"So, is this your first year as a Helping Hands adviser?" Cat asked, trying again to make polite conversation with Izzie.

"Second," Izzie said in monotone. "*Yo fui una estudiante en la programa durante me primer año en las preparatorias.* I was a student in the program my first year of high school. Then I became an adviser."

"You must really enjoy it," Cat said.

Izzie shrugged. "I do it to help educate people about my

country. Especially Americans. There's much they never care to learn about Mexico."

"I care," Cat said defensively. "That's part of why I came here. To learn about the country and culture. And to get better at my Spanish."

"*¿Por qué?*" Izzie asked. "Why do you want to get better?"

Cat smiled. She could definitely answer that question, but where should she begin? She loved Spanish—the fluidness and beauty of the language, the way the words curled in her mouth as she said them. Studying it had always been fun instead of a chore, and she wanted to speak it flawlessly. Plus, Arizona U had an amazing bilingual program she was dying to get into. If she was lucky and she improved her language skills enough, she might get a scholarship for a free ride. Then her mom and Ted would have to let her come back to Arizona for college. If it didn't cost them a dime, how could they stop her?

"Well," Cat started, suddenly dying to talk about the language she loved, "there's a college in Arizona I really want to get accepted to, and—"

"*Exactamente,*" Izzie cut her off. "To build up your school records for the university. But what does that have to do with learning about the people here?"

She stared at Cat in a silent challenge, and Cat completely blanked. Brilliant. Another strike against her, no doubt. She'd wanted to say that it was Spanish she truly loved, even more than the prospect of going to AU. It had

all sounded so much better in her head, before she'd opened her mouth…

Izzie walked through a door on the right, revealing a cheerful bedroom painted sunshine yellow. What looked most inviting about it were the two twin beds, covered in red-and-blue woven blankets. Wooden masks and woven baskets hung on the walls, right next to…a Metallica poster? A wave of relief washed over Cat as she prepared to launch her second (or was it seventh?) attempt to get on Izzie's good side.

"You like Metallica?" Cat asked eagerly.

"Sí," Izzie said flatly. *"Conocemos la música de los Estados Unidos aquí.* We *do* know your music."

"Of course you do," Cat said, backpedaling. "I didn't mean to sound like you didn't. I just meant—" She sighed, and tried again. "I love Metallica, that's all! I have all of their albums." She scrambled to search through her carry-on, and finally pulled out her iPod, triumphant. "Do you want to listen? I've got some AC/DC and Nirvana on here, too."

Izzie stared at the iPod, a mixture of longing and annoyance on her face, then shook her head. "We should get to bed. *Nos despartemas a las quatro y media mañana.*"

"We have to get up at four-thirty in the morning tomorrow?" Cat exclaimed, then silently cursed herself as Izzie rolled her eyes. She suddenly realized that flashing two-hundred-dollar electronic toys in Izzie's face and acting shocked by the idea of getting up before sunrise might not be the best way to change Izzie's "American princess" impression of her.

"You'll have to miss out on your beauty sleep," Izzie said drily. "We have work to do tomorrow."

"It's no problem. Really," Cat said. Now would be an excellent time to shut up before she made things even worse, if that was possible.

"This is your bed." Izzie motioned to her, and it was all Cat could manage to nod gratefully in her sleepiness. Her bones ached with jet lag, and her head ached from all that had happened today. She quickly laid out her clothes for the morning—a basic tee and cargo pants—sturdy and sweatproof (she hoped), then she got undressed and cleaned up in the tiny hallway bathroom. Even if she'd blown her first day with her new host sister, it was still with sheer delight and relief that she crawled between her crisp, clean sheets. Tomorrow, she'd make a fresh start with Izzie. For now, she happily closed her eyes knowing that the whole, glorious, parent-free, Boston-free summer lay stretched out before her.

Chapter Three

June 26, 5:00 A.M.

By the end of the day today, I WILL make
friends with Izzie. Either that, or I might not
live to see sunset. Izzie's loading the Jeep with
shovels and a handsaw right now. She told me
they're for working at the site, but shovels are
good for burying things, too (like bodies...). If
this is my last will and testament, I leave my

iPod and my <u>Sixteen Candles</u> DVD to Sabrina. And, Mom, if you're reading this, do NOT let Ted turn my bedroom into a study after I'm gone.

Note to Self: Next time Izzie offers you food, make sure it doesn't have antennae before eating it.

It was still pitch-dark outside as Cat dressed for her first day at the work site. She could think of only one good reason for anyone in their right mind to get up this early, and that was for a diving meet. If she'd been going to one, she would've jumped out of bed, adrenaline pumping. But as it was, she was heading out into the wilderness with Izzie for a day of hard manual labor. It wasn't the work she minded. She was looking forward to that. But Izzie was still giving her the cold shoulder, and her own patience was running short with the whole thing.

After an awkward breakfast of *bizcochos*, Mexican sweet cakes, and José's *café de olla*, coffee strong enough to wake the dead, even Abril and José must have wondered what was wrong. Izzie had talked to Abril and José, and Abril and José had talked to Cat, but Cat and Izzie hadn't said two words to each other. Then Cat had to endure Izzie's silence as they took the Canuls' Jeep to the work site.

They arrived before the other students, and as Cat took in the vacant site, she got her first inkling of how much work this summer was really going to be. The site was just beyond the edge of town, but it looked like a mini-wilderness, bordered by looming trees with heavy, junglelike vines. In the middle of it was a large, overgrown meadow strewn with thick brush, tree stumps, and rocks. There wasn't one cleared patch of ground in any direction. How was this piece of untamed land supposed to change into a school in two months' time? It didn't seem possible.

Sebastian was in the field already, along with several host parents whom Cat recognized from the welcome dinner, all laying out tools, buckets, and wheelbarrows for the day's work.

"Good morning," Sebastian called out in Spanish, walking over to them. "It's going to be hot today, so I thought we'd put the coolers in the shade." He pointed to a spot under some trees a few hundred feet away. "The Sanchez family brought the lunches, since they're helping on-site today," he told Izzie. "All you have to do is put them on ice." Then he smiled at Cat, and explained for her benefit, "Each host family takes turns preparing meals for our program."

Izzie quickly began unloading coolers filled with water bottles out of the Jeep.

"Can I help with something?" Cat offered, following her, but Izzie quickly shook her head.

"Yo lo tengo," she said as she put several packages of

food on top of the ice in the coolers. "I can take care of it."

Cat had to admire Izzie's dedication, even if the girl was being moody. Not many high schoolers she knew would give up their summer three years running to get up before dawn and work all day in the hot sun. Izzie was seriously committed. Right now, though, Cat wished she was a little *less* serious in general.

Luckily, she was rescued from Izzie's all-work, no-play attitude a few minutes later when the program bus arrived with the rest of the students. A sleepy crew of twenty students got out, and Cat, with great relief, quickly located Sabrina and Brian. Brian said a polite hello, but then walked away to join Jimmy, Rob, and Amber, three students from Beverly Hills whom Cat had met briefly at the welcome dinner. After getting a good look at their Columbia activewear, J.Crew caps, and work boots that had to cost at least a couple hundred bucks, Cat guessed they were the preppy, chronic résumé-building type. And then she blushed, remembering Izzie's reaction when she'd mentioned wanting to get better at Spanish for college. This crowd was probably just the kind that Izzie couldn't stand. But Brian had apparently hit it off with them, and Cat was glad Sabrina stuck with her instead of following Brian's lead.

"How cool is this?" Sabrina cried with a huge grin. "We're turning all of that"—she waved toward the wilderness around them—"into a school! Talk about making a

real difference. Our teachers back home were always going on and on about turning the world into a better place...yada yada. But we're actually going to do it!"

Cat grinned. "And I thought joining Greenpeace made you happy. You've reached a whole new level of eco-ecstasy."

"Hey, every hippie has her day." Sabrina laughed. "And my host family, the Domingases, couldn't be more perfect for me, either! Maria is a professor of environmental science, and Miguel is on the Oaxacan city council for civil rights. And since they don't have any kids, I have my own bathroom and bedroom!"

"This is just great," Cat groaned. "You're living with Mr. and Mrs. Peace Corps, and I end up going from one dysfunctional family right into another."

"What?" Sabrina asked. "Isn't your host family nice?"

"If 'nice' involves feeding me insects and calling me a spoiled little rich girl, I don't want to know what 'mean' is."

Sabrina's jaw dropped. "You ate insects? Poor little guys. Please tell me you didn't eat them alive or anything."

"Sabrina!" Cat sighed. "You're missing the point."

"I'm just looking out for my six-legged friends," she said. "Okay, so who's the problem?"

"My new psycho-sister," Cat started. "Izzie. She's—"

"Sabrina!" a voice suddenly called, drowning out Cat. "Come here a minute, sweets!"

They turned around to see Brian waving Sabrina over to join the J.Crew crowd.

"Be right there," Sabrina called out, then gave Cat an apologetic smile. "I really want to hear the rest of the scoop. Can it wait until later?"

Cat pasted a nonchalant smile onto her face. "Sure. Later's fine."

She tried to shrug off the deflated feeling she had as she watched Sabrina join Brian, but she managed a genuine smile only when she spotted Aidan, Pete, and Rachel walking her way.

"How's your friend and her boyfriend?" Aidan asked.

"Bordering on codependency at the moment," Cat said with a laugh.

"And the chronic sighing?"

"It's a miracle." She laughed. "I'm cured."

"That's a relief." He smiled. "Now you can enjoy the summer, right?"

Cat nodded, but before she could say anything else, Sebastian motioned everyone together. "All right, ladies and gentlemen! Let's get started." He began handing out leather work gloves and gardening tools. Some kids got shovels, others rakes or hoes, and others large hedge clippers. As Cat slipped on her gloves, Sabrina quickly reappeared at her side, with Brian in tow.

"Who was that cute stranger you were just talking to?"

Sabrina whispered, nodding toward Aidan, who was standing with Pete and Rachel a few feet away.

"His name's Aidan. I met him on the bus yesterday," Cat said, then, reading Sabrina's mind, followed it up with, "And no, I'm *not* interested, so drop the agenda, Little Miss Matchmaker."

"I don't know what you're talking about," Sabrina said innocently.

"Watch out, Cat," Brian said. "She wouldn't give up until I fell for her. She's relentless."

"Don't I know it," Cat said. And she did...way better than Brian did, too.

"In Oaxaca," Sebastian began, "hundreds of orphans live in shelters, orphanages, or homeless on the streets. Our goal is to provide them with a school that will better their chances of a brighter future. It will give them a basic start with their reading, writing, math, and science skills. This rugged field of brush you see here will, by the end of the summer, be replaced with this." He taped a poster-size paper to the side of the bus. It was a blueprint of a massive orphan school, complete with classrooms, a playground, and even a butterfly garden for interactive science and nature lessons.

"Helping Hands draws on the resources of the families and students who participate in the program. Over the course of this semester, host parents will share their talents and time with us. Many of you are living with skilled architects, others with painters, farmers, electricians, historians, or naturalists. Some host parents will help with the building of this school, and others will travel with us on our eco-educational tours to teach you about the environment, history, and cultures in this area."

Sebastian nodded toward the Sanchezes, who had joined him at the front of the group. "Señor and Señora Sanchez, Brian's host parents, will help oversee this project with me. Señor Sanchez is a contractor in Oaxaca, and he will help to make sure the foundation and structure of the building are sound. We also have three program advisers who will accompany us on all of our field trips and work with you at this site." He motioned toward Izzie, who stepped forward along with two guys Cat hadn't seen until now. "Itzel, Juan, and Carlos have grown up in Oaxaca, and they'll be able to show you around town and give you some important perspectives on our country that you won't get from the rest of us old fogies. Right, Señor Sanchez?"

"Right." Señor Sanchez laughed. "As a group," he said, picking up where Sebastian had left off, "your first task is to clear this field of rocks, trash, and brush. There are shovels and hoes to dig out tree stumps as well. Once the field is cleared, we'll level out the ground, then mark the foundation and pour it."

"I can have this whole thing cleared in fifteen minutes," Pete muttered to Cat and Rachel. "And once I'm done, the

ladies can takes turns feeling my ripped bod." With that, he dug his shovel into the ground with obvious effort, sending it a whopping two inches under the soil.

"Fifteen minutes, huh?" Rachel snickered. "Better have 'the ladies' help you."

"You'll be more productive working in pairs," Señor Sanchez continued, as if on cue, "and you'll practice your Spanish with each other while you work." He wrapped up the instructions, and everyone began pairing off.

Cat already knew what to expect from Sabrina, when she turned to her with, "Are you going to be okay finding another partner?"

"Of course," Cat said. She'd talked to Sabrina for all of about ten minutes yesterday, but this afternoon, they'd have hours to catch up. She gave Sabrina a reassuring smile. "Don't worry about me. You and Bri have fun."

"Great," Sabrina said, already walking away. "See you at lunch!"

Cat looked around to see who she could partner up with. Aidan had teamed up with Rob, and Rachel and Pete were working together. Everyone else had already paired off, too…except for Izzie. Perfect. The one person left without a partner was the one who liked her least. But she was totally out of options.

She approached Izzie, mentally preparing herself for rejection.

"Do you have a partner yet?" she asked.

Izzie hesitated, obviously trying to think of any way she might avoid answering that question. "No," she muttered.

"Can I work with you?" Cat asked. "It would only be for today, you know, if that's what you wanted."

Izzie sighed. "Yes. But we're not stopping until lunchtime." Her fiery eyes sparked. "And I don't take breaks."

"Me either," Cat said, staring Izzie down. If this was another of Izzie's tests, then Cat was more than ready to prove her wrong. She'd had enough of Izzie underestimating her. She picked up her shovel. "Just show me where to start."

As the sun climbed high in the sky, the day grew brutally hot. It wasn't the dry heat Cat had been used to in Arizona, either. This was a moist, thick heat that blanketed the site in a humid haze, making simple acts like walking feel like wading through mud. Cat carted wheelbarrow after wheelbarrow of rocks and brush to the dump truck at the edge of the site, then raked and smoothed out the ground. Thank God she'd brought her iPod along, because otherwise, the silence between her and Izzie would have been totally awkward. Instead, though, she plugged in her headphones and got lost in her music.

After the first hour of work, beads of sweat dotted her

forehead; after the second hour, her hair was damp; and after the third, she was dying for a break. But when Izzie asked her if she wanted to rest for a minute, Cat just picked up another load of rocks.

"I'm fine," she said. "Unless *you* want to stop for a while?" She stared at Izzie, waiting to see if she'd cave.

"No," Izzie said. *"Estoy bien."*

"Good," Cat said with finality. "Let's keep going."

Another two hours later, soreness had settled into her muscles, and her shirt was covered in dirt and sweat. She wasn't the only one a little worse for wear, either.

Pete and Rachel, who weighed only two hundred pounds between them, looked like they were both about to pass out. Aidan had been digging out tree stumps and shrubs for hours without stopping, and his shirt and hair were covered with twigs and dust. Sabrina's face had a radiant flush to it (she even looked good perspiring, darn her), but she looked a little worn out, too.

By the time Izzie and the other advisers passed out plates of stuffed chilies and *tortas compuestas* and water bottles to the group, everyone seemed more than ready for a lunch break. Cat had never thought water tasted so good until she put one of those cold bottles to her lips. She'd guzzled two bottles already and was sipping a third while she ate as everyone sat in companionable silence under the shady grove of trees.

"This heat is a killer," Brian said.

"Here," Sabrina said, taking off the bandana she'd tied around her hair and pouring a tiny bit of her water onto it. "Try this."

Cat watched as Sabrina rubbed Brian's forehead and neck with the wet cloth. Oh, gag. If those two got any more cuddly, she couldn't be responsible for her actions.

"Sabrina," Pete called from where he was lying in the grass under the tree, his T-shirt wrapped around his head like a turban. "You can do that to me anytime. I'm waiting, darling."

Sabrina just giggled and shook her head.

"Nice try, Petey boy." Brian snorted. He opened a water bottle and poured it out over his head. "Now, that"—he sighed—"is much better." A mischievous grin crossed his face as he dug into the cooler for another bottle.

"You know," he said, winking at Sabrina and Cat. "You girls look like you could use some cooling off, too."

Sabrina giggled.

"Oh no," Cat said, scrambling to make a getaway, "Don't even think about—"

A freezing cold spray of water hit her in the face, and Sabrina got drenched.

Rob and Jimmy got in on the act, too, and soon they'd emptied five more water bottles and everyone had gotten sprayed.

"Brian!" Cat yelled, but she was grinning in relief. The cool water felt great against her hot skin, she had to admit.

"Aren't you supposed to be *conserving* nature's resources?"

"Oh, I am," he said. "But I'm part of nature, too, and right now I need to conserve what little moisture's left in my body." He poured some more water over his head. "By adding to it." He shot another splash of water her way.

"No more!" she pleaded, giggling in spite of herself.

Giggling, that is, until she caught a glimpse of Izzie's angry face.

"That's our drinking water," Izzie said to Brian with a steely glare.

Brian laughed. "It was just a few bottles. No one's going to miss them."

"There's no other source of drinkable water here." Izzie sighed. "This water's not for wasting."

"What's the problem?" said Sebastian, walking over. He took in the scene as Izzie explained what had happened.

"We were just fooling around," Brian said.

"Itzel's right, Brian," Sebastian said in Spanish. "At home it's easy to take things like bottled water for granted, but here, we have to treat it as a necessity. The ground water's not drinkable, and bottled water isn't cheap. We have a program budget to stick to. Try to be more careful with our resources next time." He pulled out some pesos from his pocket and handed them to Brian. "About a mile down the road in town, there's a small cantina where you and Jimmy can buy some more bottles to get us through the afternoon. It shouldn't be more than a half hour's walk."

Brian stared at the pesos with a frown, but he finally nodded. And after hearing Sebastian's sobering lecture, the rest of the students quietly got up and headed back to their work. Cat helped Izzie move the coolers farther back into the shade before picking up her own shovel. Maybe she was just wiped out from working, but whatever the reason, Izzie didn't protest this time.

"Sorry about Brian and the water," Cat said to her, prepared for Izzie to launch into a tirade about spoiled Americans.

But Izzie surprised her by saying calmly, "It wasn't your fault. I just can't stand to see people being so wasteful."

Suddenly, something cold and wet hit Cat's side, making her jump. At her feet, Sabrina's drenched bandana lay dirtied on the ground. Brian was already walking down the road with Jimmy, laughing at his successful throw.

"Wait one sec, Izzie," Cat said, putting down the cooler and taking aim.

She launched a perfect curveball, hitting Brian square in the back of the neck.

"Hey!" he cried, wiping off the muddy water.

"Muy bien." Izzie laughed. "Nice aim."

Cat smiled at her. It was the first time Izzie had dropped her guard, and it was nice to see her relaxing.

"¿Te duelen?" Izzie asked, pointing at Cat's hands. "Do those hurt?"

"What?" Cat glanced down at her palms, where a row

of small blisters was forming. "I didn't even know those were there. They must be from using the shovel. I got so hot when we were working, I took my gloves off. I guess that was a bad idea." She shrugged. "I love working outside. I don't pay much attention to stuff like blisters."

"Yo tengo tiritas en el carro," Izzie said. "Those will help."

"Tiritas?" Cat asked skeptically, unable to translate the word in English and fearing another act of sabotage. "Those aren't like *chapulines,* are they?"

Izzie giggled as they reached the Jeep. "No. *Tiritas son—¿cómo se dice en ingles?*—baindawds?"

"Oh! Band-Aids!" Cat exclaimed.

"Sí," Izzie said. She pulled them out from the glove compartment and carefully wrapped them over Cat's blisters.

"Thanks," Cat said, then glanced toward the field, where everyone else was busy clearing more ground. "I guess we should get back to work."

Izzie nodded, but she hesitated. *"Lo siento por los chapulines ayer,"* she said quietly. "I'm sorry for the grasshoppers yesterday."

"No problem," Cat said, willing to forget the whole thing if she and Izzie could make their way into semi-friendship status. "But can I ask why? Don't you like being a program adviser?"

"I love helping to improve our city for my people," Izzie said. "But sometimes the students in the program aren't really here to improve things." She sighed. "The girls who came before you. In English, you call them…beaches?"

Cat had to smile at Izzie's mispronunciation of the word. "Really?"

"They didn't want to work. They just wanted to play. And in my country, people work to live. My family works to help our people survive. Those girls never understood." She took a deep breath. "I thought you were like them."

Cat looked Izzie straight in the eyes. "I don't know a lot about your country yet, but I'm hoping to learn."

"I saw how hard you worked this morning. The other girls never worked like that. They were afraid to get dirty." Izzie paused, and then she giggled. "And you *did* eat two helpings of *chapulines*. You're a fast learner."

Cat grinned. "Just don't try it again." Then she broke into laughter, too.

Izzie pointed to the iPod shuffle Cat had strapped around her arm. *"Puedo escuchar algo Metallica ahora?"* she asked tentatively.

"Of course you can listen to some. Anything for a fellow groupie." Cat grinned, handing her iPod to Izzie. She showed her how to run through the playlists, and then said, "Try the 'Gods of Metal' playlist first. It rocks."

As they walked to their workstation in the field, she was comforted by the thought that maybe there was hope for a truce with Izzie, after all.

When the work wrapped up that afternoon, Cat was sore

and dirty, but strangely content. It was the first intense workout she'd had since giving up diving, and it felt great to put her muscles to good use. And once she cleaned up, she'd finally be able to spend some time one-on-one with Sabrina. She had so much to tell her, and there was so much she wanted to hear about Scottsdale, too. She'd been looking forward to it all day.

"Are we still on for later?" Cat asked Sabrina when she found her and Brian at the bus putting their equipment away. "Maybe we could check out a few of the museums or churches to prep for our first essay. Or, just sit at a café for a while and catch up."

Sabrina grinned. "Definitely. There are a few outdoor markets I marked on my city map that I want to check out. The tribes here use all-natural dyes for their fabrics, and I want to decorate my bedroom here in all things organic."

"Impressive." Cat grinned. "You can save the planet, boost the economy, and do some interior decorating while you're at it."

"I like to call it multitasking." Sabrina laughed. "And afterward, Brian wants to stop at one of the cantinas in the *zócalo* to try something called *mezcal con gusano*. I guess that's like Oaxacan tequila."

Brian grinned. "I'm drinking down the worm and all."

"Oh." Cat's heart sank as she leaned toward Sabrina. "I thought maybe it was going to be just you and me?"

"You don't mind if he comes along, do you?" Sabrina

whispered out of Brian's earshot. "I really want you two to get to know each other better."

Cat paused, weighing her options carefully. This summer was supposed to be about having the time of their lives together, but if Sabrina stayed as fixated on Brian as she'd been so far, what were the chances of that happening? She suddenly felt the tiniest pangs of panic as she remembered that her mom had warned her about things like this happening when friends grew apart. She'd said it again just yesterday morning at the Boston airport as they waited for Cat's flight to board.

"Are you sure you want to go?" her mom had asked her for the hundredth time. "If you stayed here this summer, you'd make new friends. You could even start training for diving. There's still time to change your mind."

"Like I would give up Mexico and a summer with Sabrina to stay here. Please." Cat gave a short snort of laughter. "Not a chance."

Her mom had given her a sad, little knowing smile, the kind that she always gave when she thought Cat was about to make a mistake. "There's going to come a time in your life when you and Sabrina will go your separate ways. I know you don't believe it now, but friendships grow and change, just like people. Sabrina might have even changed since you've been away from Arizona. You never know. You'll have to say good-bye to her at summer's end, too, and it'll still hurt, Cat."

"Not as much as it'll hurt my social life to be stuck here," Cat had countered.

"All right. You win. I can't fight with you about this, and heaven forbid I should do anything else to ruin your social life. Then you'd *really* hate me forever." Her mom laughed, then hugged her. "Have a great time and give Sabrina my love. You two look out for each other."

Now Cat wondered what this summer was going to be like if their twosome turned into a permanent three. She had never worried that a guy would gain the number-one spot in Sabrina's life. But Sabrina had never dated a guy for longer than a couple of weeks before, let alone crossed international borders with one.

She knew that she should take some time to get to know Brian, especially if he meant that much to Sabrina. Still, the idea of being a third wheel made her cringe. But how could she say no to her friend?

"Cat!" a voice called out, making her and Sabrina turn. It was Izzie, walking her way. "Carlos and I were just talking with some of the other students"—she motioned to where Aidan, Pete, and Rachel were standing in a small huddle—"and they want to do some research for their first papers. We're going to show them some of Oaxaca this afternoon, if you want to come along."

Cat hesitated. Now what? Izzie had just given her the perfect out. Pete and Rachel were quirky but fun, and

Aidan seemed like someone she might become real friends with. But was it totally snarky of her to blow off Sabrina and Brian? In a matter of seconds, Sabrina made the decision for her.

"You should go with them," Sabrina said, and when Cat started to protest, she interrupted her. "We have all summer for girl bonding." Then she leaned toward Cat. "In case it has escaped your attention, Aidan is hot. *And* he does not seem to have a girlfriend. At least not one who's here. He has great summer-fling potential."

"You mean the summer fling I'm definitely *not* having?" Cat said drily.

"The right guy, the right moment, and you'll cave," Sabrina said confidently. "Now go!" She gave her a playful shove.

"Okay, okay," Cat said, laughing. It was one of the things she loved about Sabrina—her ability to simplify just about any dilemma, even if half the time she was slightly off base in her well-intentioned good deeds.

"What did Sabrina mean when she called Aidan 'hot'?" Izzie asked as she and Cat left to go home and clean up. "We've all been working in the sun, and he's not even sweating."

"No," Cat said, smiling. "'Hot' in English can mean handsome, too."

Izzie smiled. *"Es verdad. Él es un taco de ojo."*

Cat giggled. "An eye taco? Do I even want to know what that means?"

"Muy guapo," Izzie tried again. "Pleasing to the eye."

"In the States, we call that 'eye candy.'" Cat said, bursting out laughing. Then she blushed. "Not that *I* think he is... eye candy, I mean. Just because you and Sabrina gave him the same rating doesn't mean I agree."

"But you have all summer to change your mind," Izzie said with an impish grin.

That afternoon, Cat and Izzie met up with Carlos, Aidan, Pete, and Rachel in the *zócalo*. After buying some churros to munch on, they made their way to a modest, bright blue house with a small tiled plaque hanging outside.

"It's La Casa de Juarez," Izzie told them, nodding toward the plaque. "This is where Benito Juárez, the greatest president of Mexico, lived in the early 1800s."

"*One* of the greatest," Carlos said, giving Izzie a teasing smile. "Itzel just loves the revolutionaries."

"Pues, él fue un hombre fantástico," Izzie said defensively. "He was a poor orphan, but he was raised by priests to become a great fighter for agricultural reform and Indian rights. He believed in equality for every person."

Cat followed Izzie and everyone else inside the humble house, where a display gave some information on Benito's background. They wandered through the rooms, studying the simple furnishings and artwork. It took only about fif-teen minutes to tour the entire house, small as it was.

"It's hard to believe a man could start out with so little," Rachel remarked, "and become the president of a whole country."

"We had a president like that, too," Cat said. "Abraham Lincoln."

Izzie nodded, her eyes lighting up passionately. "Sometimes Benito is called the Lincoln of Mexico." She paused in front of a small portrait of a woman with dark hair and intelligent eyes hanging on the sitting room wall. "This is Benito's wife, Margarita Maza. In English, she would have been called...a feemaneest?"

"You mean a feminist?" Cat asked.

Izzie nodded. "Margarita was white, and twenty years younger than Benito," she said. "She became a revolution-ary just by marrying him. And even though they lived apart in exile for years, they were known to have loved each other until they died."

Cat snorted. "Yeah, right. That would never happen nowadays. That kind of love doesn't exist anymore."

Aidan started, "Hey, behind every great man—"

"*Beside* every great man," Izzie corrected him, "is a greater woman." She grinned at Cat, who laughed.

"Now *that* I believe," Cat said.

"*Ven conmigo,*" Izzie said as they left the museum,

motioning for them to follow her down the street. "There's another great woman I want to show you."

A few minutes later, they were standing in front of the Basilica de Soledad, a massive Baroque-style church with a creamy stone facade.

"It means our lady of solitude," Carlos explained as they quietly entered the church. "According to legend, the Virgin Mary chose our city as one in which she should be honored. In 1620, a caravan camped outside the city discovered one extra mule no one could remember bringing along. Inside the mule's pack was a statue of the Virgin. As of that day, she became the patron saint of Oaxaca, and this basilica was built in her honor. It's the religious center of our city."

Inside, the church was awe-inspiring, with gold-leaf gilding everywhere Cat looked. But what amazed her was the statue of the Virgin herself. She was larger than life, enshrined in a huge glass case, her pale, somber face peering out from a floor-length cloak that sparkled with gems.

"Are those diamonds?" Aidan asked.

"Sí," Izzie replied. *"Hay seiscientos.* Six hundred."

"That's some serious bling," Cat said in awe.

"Has anyone ever tried to steal her cloak?" Rachel asked.

"She is far too revered for that," Carlos said. "Villagers

walk for miles to come pray near her. Sometimes, they even come barefoot because they have no shoes."

"Why is she called the lady of solitude?" Pete asked.

"For the nights of solitude she spent mourning between Christ's crucifixion and resurrection," she explained.

Cat kept staring at *la virgen*, even after Carlos led the rest of the group to the front of the basilica. From her massive gold crown to her stately black velvet cape—every aspect of *la virgen* was evidence of how well she was loved by the Oaxacans.

"She's amazing," a voice said beside her, and it was only then that Cat noticed that Aidan was still there admiring the statue, too. "I can't imagine something this rich in St. Patrick's Cathedral," he said, "and St. Patrick's is pretty impressive to begin with."

"Is that in New York?" Cat asked.

Aidan nodded. "You've never been?"

"Not to Manhattan," Cat said. "I haven't seen much of the East Coast."

"Where are you from?" Aidan asked.

Cat laughed, knowing what she said next was going to sound ridiculous. "Just outside of Boston, but only since about three months ago. Before that, Arizona."

Aidan laughed. "I've never heard 'Boston' said like it was a curse word before, except when the Yankees play the Red Sox."

"I'm not a big fan," Cat said.

"Of the Sox or of Boston?"

"Both."

Aidan grinned. "I'm with you on the Sox. But Boston's a pretty cool city. I've been a few times. What school do you go to?"

"North Harbor High," Cat said.

"Well, that settles it," Aidan said with mock seriousness. "We can *never* be friends now."

"Why not?"

"Because you attend the school of my arch-nemesis, Scott Thurgood. He killed me in a breaststroke relay last spring at regionals. North Harbor has one of the best swimming and diving programs in the Northeast."

"Hey, I didn't get to pick my school." Cat laughed. "Don't hold it against me."

Aidan grinned. "All right, but promise me if you ever see Scott Thurgood, you'll tell him that next year at the northeast finals, he's at my mercy."

"Sure thing." Cat smiled. "So, what's your time classification?"

"4A," Aidan said shyly. "How do you know about swimming classifications? Are you a swimmer, too?"

"Nah," Cat said. "I had friends in Scottsdale on the swim team. They're not 4A's though. You must be great."

Aidan shrugged. "I'm just a total sucker for the water. I usually spend every summer lifeguarding at the Jersey shore, and I want to be an oceanographer someday."

"I love the ocean, too," Cat said, her heart thumping with excitement. It was on the tip of her tongue to mention her diving. It could be so great to talk to him about meets, especially now that her old diving buds Sam, Jason, and Nikki had virtually dropped off the face of the earth. She could pick his brain for stats, too, since diving and swim teams had meets together. He'd be bound to know some of the regional divers. But then she reminded herself that she wasn't a diver...not anymore.

"If you love the ocean," Aidan said, "you've probably been to the New England Aquarium in Boston already. Isn't it awesome? Four stories of underwater viewing."

"I haven't been there yet," Cat said. She hadn't even known there was an aquarium in Boston—and four stories of it! She could spend days there if she went...which she wasn't planning to do. "My parents have toured the city a few times," she said with an indifferent shrug, "but I haven't been that into it."

Aidan looked at her with the tiniest hint of skepticism. "For somebody who hasn't lived in Boston long, you sound pretty down about it."

Cat paused, and then flushed. She had to admit, it didn't sound logical. But how could she explain to him all the things she already hated about the city? Nothing felt right in Boston, not like it had in Arizona. Her mom had kept telling her to give it time—she'd learn to love Boston, and

maybe even come to like Ted, too, if she kept the right attitude. But the right attitude never showed up. Her mom had said Boston was beautiful, but her mom had said nothing about the blizzards that had welcomed them to the city, even though it was already March! Not to mention something called "windchill" that Cat found out meant freeze-any-exposed-parts-of-your-body cold. For the first couple of months, Cat's new bedroom, which the previous owners had painted beige (ick!), looked out on a gray winter sky, fifteen-foot snowdrifts, and leafless trees.

Her mom had said that Boston schools were some of the best in the country, but her mom obviously knew nothing about the social disaster that resulted from switching schools halfway through junior year. Cat had found herself surrounded by crewneck sweaters and loafers—no sandals or summery tank tops. On top of that, there was this whole clique thing she didn't have the first clue how to decipher, so her old friends dwindled, and no new ones took their place. There were so many reasons why she already hated Boston, where did she even start?

"I never wanted to move to Boston in the first place," she told Aidan. "My parents made me. But I'm moving back to Arizona as soon as I graduate next year."

"I hate it when the 'rents make executive decisions like that," he said. "But, hey, you still have to survive a year there before your emancipation, right?"

Cat laughed. "Sad, but true."

Aidan opened up what looked like a sketchbook that he was carrying. "I'm starting a list for you," he said, writing on a blank page. "The Best of Boston. Maybe it'll kill some of the time for you. It beats dying of boredom. Besides, if you *look* like you're busy, maybe your parents won't ever force you to do something really cheesy, like reenacting the Boston Tea Party by throwing fake bags of tea into the harbor."

"I take it you're speaking from personal experience?" Cat asked.

Aidan nodded, then shuddered. "Family bonding at the Boston Tea Party Museum. It wasn't pretty."

"I can only imagine." Cat laughed.

As she and Aidan caught up with the rest of the group, Cat rolled the idea of sightseeing in Boston around in her head. The more she thought about it, the more reasons she came up with for why she shouldn't. Visiting the aquarium would be cool, but, then again, why should she waste her time in the city when she'd be there for only a year? Plus, her mom and Ted would get all excited if she got touristy, thinking she was finally "fitting in" to her new home and life. Which was *so* not true. Aidan's to-do list made sense, if she wanted to give the city a genuine try. But she didn't. Not now, not in the fall when she got home. Not ever.

Chapter Four

Cat stared at the sculpture of the female mannequin in front of her, pretending to be fascinated, all the while racking her brain for a way to get Sabrina and Brian out of the Canuls' art gallery ASAP. They'd stopped here after a trip to the Museum of Contemporary Art, and from the minute they'd walked into the gallery a half hour ago, things had gone from *mal* to *muy mal* to *horrible*. Cat was pretty sure that if she couldn't get Brian out the door soon, Izzie was going to completely lose it.

Since her arrival on Sunday, Cat had spent nearly every

afternoon exploring the city with Izzie and the other advisers from the program. The program had had a few organized tours of the city, too, but Cat wanted to see more in
her free time. It seemed like a great way to improve her
Spanish, and Cat was relishing speaking it whenever she
could. Sometimes Aidan, Pete, and Rachel joined the
group for tours, and today—shocker—even Sabrina and
Brian had tagged along for a research trip to the Museum
of Contemporary Art. The museum was on the checklist of
mandatory sights to see in their spare time, and they'd be
tested on some of the artwork on their midterm and final.
Most of their program essays would be about one of the
eco-tours, but since they hadn't been on any yet,
Sebastian had left this first essay open-ended, and Cat
had decided to write her first paper on the influence of
tribal folk art on contemporary Oaxacan artists. Izzie had
suggested that she start her research at the museum,
since many well-known artists exhibited work there.

During the museum tour, Cat was relieved to see
Sabrina and Izzie hitting it off. Brian, on the other hand,
spent about five minutes total in the museum. He breezed
through the paintings, scribbling quick notes that he said
would help him "ace the exams." Once he'd gotten all the
info, he called it quits. "I need some fresh air," he said.
"The rain forest canopy tour we're taking next Saturday?
That's way more my style. All this stuff looks like finger

painting to me after a while." He laughed and took a seat outside in the sculpture garden to wait for the girls to finish the museum tour.

Izzie hadn't said one word, but Cat could tell from her tight-lipped silence and crossed arms that she didn't take too well to anyone criticizing her country's artwork. After they finished up at the museum, Izzie invited them back to her parents' gallery to see art from the local tribes, and that's when the real trouble started.

"Buenas tardes," Abril had greeted them when they stepped into the cheerful gallery with salmon-pink walls. *"Quieren ver nuestros artistas.* So you want to see our artists. *¡Muy bueno!"*

José gave them a quick tour. "In the back are the *alebrijes,* wood carvings made by the Zapotec tribes. The carvings are of imaginary creatures that represent the spirit of Oaxaca." He motioned to shelves along one wall holding ornate vases and pots. "Here's the black pottery and orange pottery of the Mixtecs. And on the other side of the gallery are the paintings and sculptures."

Brian and Sabrina headed for the paintings first, while Cat took in the intricate *alebrijes*—magical horselike beings with wings, fire-breathing lizardlike creatures with feathers, and animals that looked sort of like giraffes, or gryphons, or dragons. They were an imaginative mixture of tails, beaks, and wings, and were so beautiful. She slowly made her way through the rest of the gallery, admiring the watercolor and oil paintings along the walls, until a large sculpture standing alone in the middle of a smaller room caught her eye. It was a see-through female torso, filled, top to bottom, with bloody mannequin hands. It was unsettling to look at, and unlike anything she'd ever seen before.

"If the world weren't so full of violence," Sabrina said, walking over with Brian and Izzie to inspect the sculpture, "no one would ever have to create art like that."

"That's not art." Brian laughed. "It's Barbie meets *Texas Chainsaw Massacre*."

"Brian!" Sabrina giggled. "Indigenous artwork is nothing to make fun of." But she scolded him with about as much anger as a butterfly.

Just hearing Sabrina's cooing tone irritated Cat. If anyone else had made the comment Brian had, Sabrina would have jumped down their throat. But Sabrina, usually so outspoken about tolerance and multicultural education, had become eager to please around Brian. She hadn't stood up for her beliefs around him once on this trip.

So to prove a point, Cat said, "I think the sculpture's cool. Maybe it's about the exploitation of women or something." She glanced at Izzie, who, judging by her frown, hadn't found Brian's comment so funny either.

"*Es arte muy importante,*" Izzie said, staring furiously at

Brian. "It's a piece by Diego Lopez, one of our local artists. The torso is Mexico, and the hands symbolize the toil and bloodshed of the common man's battle for independence and reform."

"I like my interpretation better," Brian teased, but Izzie didn't crack even the smallest smile, and Cat saw the color rising in her cheeks. Izzie was so passionate about her country, and Brian just seemed to like getting her fired up. How had he ever been elected student-body president at his high school? He sure didn't have a great appreciation for the "common man," or his plight.

Now, as Cat stared at the sculpture, she knew what she had to do. It was time to plan a retreat before an all-out war was declared. She'd have to come back to the Canuls' gallery later, on her own, to study more of the pieces for her paper.

"Is anyone else hungry?" she asked, breaking the awkward silence that had settled over them since Brian's last remark. "I've had a craving for flan all day." Flan, she had discovered earlier in the week, was Mexico's next best thing to cheesecake—a custardy caramel dessert that melted in her mouth. True, she wasn't hungry, but she was hoping Brian would be. And she was right, because he piped up with, "I'm up for some grub."

Izzie's anger seemed to dim a little, too, and she gave a small smile. "I know something that's even better than flan, and the perfect place for it. Have you ever heard of *xocoatl*?"

"Chocolate?" Cat said in disbelief. "*Xocoatl* is chocolate?"

"Mexico's finest," Izzie said with a grin. "The word 'chocolate' comes from the Aztec word *'xocoatl.'* It was their word for a drink they made from the cacao tree."

"Hot chocolate," Cat guessed.

Izzie nodded. "They liked it so much, it was used in offerings to the deities, and even in marriage ceremonies. In Mesoamerica, it wasn't called the food of the gods for nothing."

They were sitting at an outdoor table at Hotel Chocolate Posada on Fco. Javier Mina, which Izzie kept referring to as "chocolate street." Even the air was filled with the sweet aroma of it, wafting from the chocolate mills scattered along the street. Cat and Sabrina were looking over a menu, which contained countless hot chocolate and chocolate snack choices, all of which looked delicious.

A young, beautiful waitress with bright green eyes and raven hair stopped at their table to get their order, and as she walked away, Brian gave a low whistle.

"Now she's what I call fine art," he said with a mischievous grin.

"Brian!" Sabrina giggled, slapping his arm playfully. "Behave."

Cat exchanged a look of exasperation with Izzie. As the drinks arrived, she wondered just how genuine Brian's interest in the community and environment was, when today he seemed more interested in the "scenery." He put up a good front most days, working just as hard as everyone else at the work site, but it came across as a little too sugarcoated. Sabrina was completely love struck, though, and Cat hoped he wasn't quite as one-dimensional as he seemed, especially for Sabrina's sake.

The next afternoon, with her notes from the museum and the gallery laid out across her bed, Cat decided to take a stab at her essay. She managed to type some stilted sentences onto her laptop, but she was having trouble remembering how to spell the simplest Spanish phrases. She could hear the Spanish words in her head. Their soft lilts and trilled *r*'s always formed easily and flawlessly when she said them, but the second she tried to type them, she was at a loss. Not being able to study the language in Boston this past semester had made her lose so much of her Spanish, and it made her heartsick. She loved this language, but she couldn't even do it justice in a simple essay.

"Is *'pintura'* spelled with an *i* or an *e*?" she asked Izzie.

"*Con un i*," Izzie answered, glancing up from a biography of Cesar Chávez.

Cat grinned, looking at Izzie's bopping head and tapping feet. She was surprised Izzie could hear her at all over the headphones she'd had on for the last two hours. Since she'd introduced Izzie to it, the girl had become iPod obsessed. And leave it to Izzie to jam to Def Leppard and read Chávez's bio at the same time. Izzie had told her that she tried to read one biography of an important Hispanic historical figure every month as a way of honoring her country's people. And revolutionary metal, Izzie'd explained, was the perfect mood music for such deep reading. Right now, Cat wished it was the perfect mood music for essay writing, too, but, sadly, wailing guitars, as much as she loved them, weren't conducive to literary genius.

She typed two more words, then stopped. "Is there an accent over the *o* in *'Iona'*?"

"No, no accent," Izzie said patiently.

"Thanks," Cat said. She'd already asked Izzie at least ten times for the correct spellings for words, and she was only two pages into the essay. This could take all day. She flipped over on her bed and sighed. "I definitely need a break."

"But you only just started," Izzie said in Spanish. She pulled off Cat's headphones and held them out to her. "Do you want to listen to your music?"

"No, you keep listening," Cat said. It was the least she could do for Izzie since she was helping her with this painful essay. "I need to focus anyway. How will I be able

to study Spanish in college if I can't write basic sentences?" She sighed. "The AU admissions people will take one look at my GPA and sample essay and they'll think, Not only does this girl write Spanish worse than a two-year-old, but she's no brain in her other courses either. My application will go straight into the trash." She moaned. "This is my payback for letting my other grades drop this semester. Now I suck at my favorite subject, too!"

"Why did you let your grades drop?" Izzie asked.

"The scare factor," Cat said, and then, when Izzie looked at her blankly, added, "I was hoping if I flunked out, my mom would let me move back to Arizona." Cat laughed. "But I couldn't even make myself flunk! I've never gotten an F on anything in my life. The worst I could do was go from an A average to a C."

"And what did your mom do then?" Izzie asked.

"She got me a tutor."

Izzie laughed. "Your mom is one smart woman."

"Tell me about it." Cat sighed. "I wish she'd gotten me Spanish lessons instead. I would gladly have taken those."

She stared at the blinking cursor on her laptop, her fingers poised over the keys. But only one Spanish word popped up in her head—a big fat *nada*. She closed her Word document. She'd deal with it later…after she checked e-mail, downloaded some iTunes onto her computer, wrote her daily update in her journal, and washed her hair. Yeah, maybe after all that. She logged in to her e-mail and found a message from her mom:

To: lilmermaid@email.com
From: born2teach@email.com
Subject: Missing you in Boston

Hi sweetie,

I'm glad you're enjoying your first week in Mexico. Señora Canul dropped me an e-mail yesterday to tell us how much they're enjoying having you as a houseguest. She sounds lovely, and so does Itzel. How nice for you to have a sister for the summer!

Ted says hello, and he wants to know if you've tried any cactus juice. He had some once when he was in Cabo San Lucas and loved it. By the way, I know your birthday is a couple of weeks away, and I won't be able to make your traditional birthday cheesecake for you this year. Is there something else you want or need for your summer? Let us know.

Caitlin, honey, I've attached a letter to this e-mail. But before you read it, I want you to know that Ted and I DID NOT ask Coach Landon to send it. He didn't have your e-mail address, so he sent it to Ted's, but the letter is for you. All we ask is that you read it and give it some thought.

Lots of love,

Mom

Cat stared at the screen for a long minute before clicking on the attachment. When she did, a letter from Coach Landon popped up, along with the diving-meet and training schedule for the fall. "Just in case you change your mind," Coach Landon wrote. "You'd be a great asset to the club and varsity teams."

She reread the letter, getting madder by the second. Finally, she hit Delete and slammed the lid of her laptop closed.

"Everything okay?" Izzie asked.

"Fine," Cat mumbled, grabbing her international cell phone off the dresser. Her mom had rented one for her, but it was for emergency use only. And this was definitely an emergency. She'd programmed in Sabrina's international cell number earlier in the week, and now she punched in a text message to her.

> **KitCat:** U there?
> **Rina:** Sí
> **KitCat:** Can we meet? It's an ER.

Cat waited, expecting a message from Sabrina to pop up right away. After all, she'd used "ER," their code for dramas of a serious nature. Finally, after several endless minutes, another message blipped onto her phone screen.

> **Rina:** I'm out w/Bri. Sorry. Call u l8r?

Cat stared at the screen. Never, in all their years of friendship, had Sabrina ever postponed an emergency meeting for a guy. *Especially* for a guy!

KitCat: K. Bye.

She jammed her cell phone into her pocket and grabbed her journal off her bed.

"I'm going for a walk," Cat said to Izzie. She'd head to the *zócalo* and find a café where she could write for a while. Normally when she felt this way, she'd head for the pool and channel some of that anger into diving and swimming laps. As a stress reliever, journal writing came in a lousy second, but her options were pretty limited.

"Are you sure everything is all right?" Izzie asked, genuine concern shining in her normally fiery eyes.

Cat paused in the doorway. Sabrina was the only person she'd ever talked to about family stuff, but since Sabrina didn't want to listen right this second...

"I just got an unbelievable e-mail from my mom," Cat said finally. "It's some stuff I'm dealing with at home..." She sighed. This was hard to explain without telling the whole family saga from the beginning. If this was going to be a long discussion, they might as well be having it outside in the sunshine. "Want to come on a walk with me?"

"Sure," Izzie said. "There's a place I can show you that might cheer you up."

As they walked through the streets, Cat vented. She didn't even realize she'd been speaking fluid Spanish the entire time, until Izzie laughed.

"Dios mío," Izzie said, smiling broadly. "And my parents think I talk fast. You speak my language way better than you write it."

Cat blushed. "Actually, sometimes I can speak it faster than English."

Fast was right. It had only taken Cat about five blocks to fill Izzie in on her parents' divorce and her mom's remarriage to Ted. She left out the diving part of the story, though. She was afraid if she talked about it, she'd start missing it more, and she really didn't want to deal with an onslaught of questions about why she quit. Her parents' nonstop nagging was bad enough.

"So," Izzie said. "This Ted. Does he treat your mom badly?"

"No," Cat said, surprised at the question. She thought about the last few months in Boston—how often she'd heard her mother laughing in the kitchen with Ted while they made dinner, or smiling as she read a card he'd surprised her with. "He treats her really great. I think he probably loves her."

"¿Y tú?" Izzie asked. "Does he treat you badly?"

"No, no," Cat said. "He's…very polite to me. Friendly, I guess." True, they hadn't spent much time together without her mom around, but Ted had always tried to include her in conversations at the dinner table and had invited her on numerous "family outings." *She* had been the one who had chosen to stay in her room instead of joining them. Ted had even come to a few of her diving meets in Arizona, before the move.

"If he's nice to you and your mom," Izzie said, "why don't you like him?"

"Because," Cat started, then paused.

Because he made her move to Boston. Because he married her mom. Because…he wasn't her dad. Because her *dad* should've been the one to make her mom happy. Because her *dad* should've been the one to stick around so Cat never would've had to move to Boston in the first place.

There were so many reasons running through her head, but when she thought of how they'd sound if she said them, she couldn't. None of them seemed fair to Ted, and all of them suddenly sounded childish, even to her.

"I don't know," Cat said finally. "I just don't like him, that's all." What was she, five years old? That wasn't a reason, that was a pathetic attempt to drop the subject. But Izzie thankfully took the hint as, just then, they stopped in front of a run-down building that had the word "*Orfanato*" written across the top. Children were playing on the steps outside, and when they saw Izzie, they ran to her, calling her name excitedly.

"They know you," Cat said.

Izzie nodded. "I volunteer at this orphanage during the school year, but in the summers I take off to work with Helping Hands instead. These children are the ones we're building the school for." She scooped up one small girl, who threw her arms affectionately around Izzie's neck. "This little girl, Esperanza, has never met her father. And Pedro,"—she nodded to a little boy sucking his thumb on the stairway—"his parents abandoned him. These children have no family. They aren't as lucky as me...or you."

Cat shifted her eyes away from Izzie, feeling the slightest bit uncomfortable, and instead watched the children playing. They were smiling and laughing with Izzie, and Cat could tell Izzie enjoyed spending time with them, too. A little while later, Izzie said her good-byes and she and Cat made their way home. As they walked, Cat thought about the orphans. The simple fact was that, even as screwed up as it felt at the moment, at least she *had* a family. But that still didn't mean she had to like the one she'd gotten stuck with.

Chapter Five

July 7, 8:00 A.M.

Note to Self: The next time a best friend tells you that she has time for you *and* her boyfriend, don't hold your breath, or block out your calendar.

The next Saturday morning, the Helping Hands group left for their first eco-excursion to the cloud forests north of Oaxaca. When Cat stepped on board the bus, she saw Sabrina sitting at the back, cuddled up with Brian—the

norm these days. So when Izzie picked seats for her and Cat up front, Cat didn't protest. She was still mad at the way Sabrina had blown her off yesterday, and she wanted to make sure Sabrina knew it. It didn't take long for the guilt factor to set in. Only minutes after the bus pulled out of Oaxaca, Sabrina appeared in the aisle beside Cat.

"Hey, KitCat," she said. "Guess what? Maria, my host mom, is coming along today to give the lecture on the cloud forest. I can't wait! I've already learned a ton about conservation efforts from her. She even has a connection in the environmental law department at AU who she wants me to meet when I get back home."

"That's great," Cat said flatly, keeping her eyes focused on the seat in front of her.

"Hey," Sabrina said. "How come you didn't return my phone calls last night?"

"Oh, you called?" Cat asked nonchalantly, playing stupid. The five voice mails Sabrina had left on her cell had not escaped her attention. "Izzie and I went for a walk, and I forgot to take my cell with me."

"Oh," Sabrina said, her eyes wavering uncertainly. "Okay. I just wanted to make sure you were all right. What happened?"

Cat shrugged. "Nothing much. I freaked about some family stuff, but it's all good now." Lie, lie, *lie*. She was dying to spill everything to Sabrina, but she also wanted to give her a little dig for leaving her high and dry. This was not one of her better sides—this stubborn desire to retaliate. But right now, she didn't feel like being an "understanding" friend—especially if it involved trying to understand Sabrina's current boy addiction.

A questioning and slightly dismayed look crossed Sabrina's face, but she sighed and said, "Okay. But if you want to talk later, I'm here."

Cat watched her walk back to Brian as a pang of guilt settled deep in her stomach. She was mad at Sabrina, but rubbing it in hadn't made her feel much better. She certainly didn't want to spend the summer playing silly payback games with her friend. She'd have to fix things with her later.

She sighed and looked out the window at the winding road they were taking up into the mountains. The farther away from Oaxaca they got, the denser the trees grew, until they bent over the roadway in heavy, jungle masses. Cat had never seen such vibrant greens, especially since the hills of Arizona stayed a crackled brown for most of the year. After a couple hours on the road, the bus stopped in the tiny village of Benito Juárez, named after Mexico's famous president, nestled high in the Sierra del Norte and surrounded by thick forests of pine oak. When Cat stepped off the bus with Izzie, she was met with a breathtaking view of the mountains spreading out all around, a dense cloud cover combing their peaks and sweeping into their valleys and crevices.

Sebastian introduced Maria Domingas to the group, and Cat saw a woman who could have been a slightly older, but no less beautiful, version of Sabrina step forward. Her skin was darker than Sabrina's, and she had glossy black hair, but she wore a neatly tailored safari-style jacket and pants that would have been right up Sabrina's alley (if they were organically made, of course).

"Cloud forests," she began, smiling at the students, "are a very special type of rain forest. They occur only at high altitudes and are covered with low-lying cloud banks up to eighty percent of the time. Humidity levels in these forests are one hundred percent most days, and the constant supply of aboveground water makes them an ideal environment for lush vegetation and animal life."

"What types of animals?" Aidan asked, pulling out his study guide to take notes.

"There are thousands of species of birds, plants, and animals here," Maria said. "And the people who spend time researching these forests every day continually discover new insect species."

As Maria gave an overview of the plants and animals, the students made their way into the forest toward the starting point for the canopy tour. It was a short hike through dense ground sprouting ferns and thick moss, and with every step, Cat grew more excited. The damp air smelled sweet and rich with growing things, and she couldn't wait to get a better view of the forest from the treetops. Several nature guides were waiting for the group at the start of the trail, next to a complex series of dangling ropes and pulleys that stretched high into the treetops, ready to lift the students, one by one, straight up into the clouds.

Brian was the first in line to get his rope harness fitted by Amaranta, a very fit guide with very short shorts.

"You can tie me up any day," Brian said, to which Jimmy and Rob cracked up laughing, and Amaranta blushed and giggled.

Cat rolled her eyes and looked around for Sabrina, hoping that she hadn't heard that remark. Even if it was a joke…talk about tacky. But Sabrina was hanging back toward the very end of the line, and Cat could tell from the look on her face that she wasn't hearing much of anything. Instead, she was staring at the rope-and-pulley system in the treetops and turning several shades paler. Brian noticed Sabrina's pasty-white face, too.

"Are you okay?" he asked Sabrina, but Cat knew that she wasn't. If Sabrina actually managed to make it up to the treetops, Cat seriously doubted she'd be able to stay up there without passing out. The girl hated heights of any kind. She wouldn't even climb the jungle gym when they were kids, for crying out loud. But Cat doubted Brian knew anything about it, since Sabrina had sworn her to secrecy about it years ago.

"I—I'm just not feeling too well," Sabrina said. "Headache."

"Maybe you should sit this one out," Cat said sympathetically, all of her earlier anger toward Sabrina forgotten. This was her best friend, and she wasn't about to let her risk fainting a hundred feet aboveground, even if she *was* boy crazy at the moment.

"But Maria will be so disappointed," she started. "She was so excited about showing me this."

"She'll understand," Cat said.

Sabrina finally nodded and, after checking with Sebastian and Maria, said she was going to walk back to the village. "I'll wait for you guys there."

Brian cast a look of longing up to the treetops, and then said flatly, "I could come with you, if you want."

Cat almost rolled her eyes. At least he was trying to be a gentlemen, but it was totally obvious that he'd much rather spend the next few hours on the canopy tour than with Sabrina.

"I'll stay," Cat said with finality.

Sabrina laughed. "Neither one of you is going to stay. You have to take notes for the next essay. And it's only a headache. I'll be perfectly fine. Besides, hanging out with the villagers will be fun. Maybe I'll learn how to grow my own food or something."

Brian didn't hesitate for another second before kissing Sabrina's cheek and hurriedly getting in line with Rob and

Jimmy to be next up into the trees. He gave a Tarzan yell
as he was pulled up into the canopy, which was followed
by an audible scolding from Sebastian. Cat offered one
more time to stay behind, but Sabrina was adamant. She
would go back to the village alone, and that was that.

Cat watched her leave, then turned back to get in line
for the rope seat. But everyone else had already gone
ahead, except for Aidan, who seemed, surprisingly, to be
waiting for her.

"Why didn't you go with everyone else?" Cat asked.

"Izzie was worried about leaving you behind, but she
was already up at the front of the line when you went to
check on Sabrina. I was at the back, so I told her I'd wait
for you."

"Thanks," Cat said, feeling her heart quicken just a
touch.

The nature guide strapped Cat into the harness of the
rope pulley, and when Amaranta gave the signal, Cat was
lifted swiftly up through the cool mountain air. A walkway
appeared through the swirling fog, suspended with ropes
and winding through the treetops, and another set of pulleys deftly swung Cat onto it, with Aidan following right
behind. After she'd regained her balance, Cat took in the
scenery around her. Aside from the distant voices of the
rest of the group echoing faintly every now and then, the
cloud forest was peacefully quiet, and so beautiful. Heavy
ferns dripping with dew hung from the trees, and flecks of

brilliant color from orchids growing out of tree trunks spotted the milky-green horizon.

"Wow," Cat whispered. A sudden rustle in the branches above her made her jump, and she teetered on the edge of the walkway, nearly losing her balance.

A pair of warm hands caught her around the waist. "I've got you," Aidan said.

"Thanks." Cat stepped back, flustered. "I'm fine now."

Aidan dropped his hands quickly, shifting his gaze from her face to the trees.

"It was a howler monkey," he said, checking the section on rain forests in their study guide. He pointed through the branches, and as Cat watched, a small, inquisitive monkey face, well camouflaged against the dark forest shadows, came into view. Then two more even smaller faces appeared beside it.

"She has babies," Cat said.

"Good eye," Aidan said, pulling out his sketchbook and scribbling away.

Cat peeked over his shoulder and saw a monkey taking shape on the paper.

"That looks just like the real thing," she said. "Do you like to draw?"

"I'm not much of an artist, really," Aidan said. "But I like to sketch animals."

Soon, they left the monkeys behind and walked farther up the path to a point where they had to "leap" from one tree walkway to another by latching their harnesses onto a rope and sliding along it. As she swung out into the air, far below her, Cat could see thick forest vegetation. She shimmied through the trees, a thrill running through her as her muscles worked to pull herself across. She was loving every minute of this.

Once she'd reached the other side, she watched Aidan nimbly make his way across. If he swam as agilely as he climbed trees, his breaststroke must be amazing to watch. She bet he could put most of the Scottsdale swim team to shame.

"You're a natural," Cat said to him once he'd landed on the platform.

"You're not too shabby yourself," Aidan said appreciatively. "I know a few guys who couldn't climb that."

"They must not eat their Wheaties." Cat laughed. She gazed out at the leafy canopy. "Everything here looks very fragile."

Aidan nodded. "It is," he said. "All these forests are dying out because of farmers clearing the land for fields and development. I did this biosphere science project last year for my bio class, where I tried to simulate the conditions in a rain forest." He laughed. "After one week, the whole thing looked like the Sahara Desert."

"But aren't they protecting tropical forests like this now?" Cat asked.

"Sure," he said. "But some species aren't strong enough

to survive after deforestation. It's happening in the oceans, too. Manatees were almost completely extinct a few years back, but they're making a comeback now." He grinned and opened his sketchbook again. "Speaking of which, I'm adding a footnote to your Best of Boston list. Go to manatee exhibit at New England Aquarium."

"That list is going to be so long, it'll take me years to see everything on it," Cat said.

"You do need to stay busy for a whole year until you can get back to Arizona, right?" Aidan smiled. "And you never know, you might even start to like Boston."

"Not likely," Cat said.

"Did you have a traumatic experience there or what?" he asked. "Sometime, I'd love to know what you've got against the place."

"How long have you got?" Cat teased.

"All day." Aidan grinned. "I'm on a walkway a hundred feet aboveground with only one exit. Do I look like I have anywhere to go?"

"All right, but don't say I didn't warn you." Cat smiled. "There'll be no escaping if you get bored."

"If I get bored," Aidan said, looking over the railing, "I'll make a jump for it." He laughed at Cat's eye roll, then said, "I won't get bored."

She began talking awkwardly at first, feeling a little self-conscious about discussing family problems with a guy she'd known for only a couple weeks. She'd felt foolish after talking to Izzie about Ted and Boston, because Izzie's world was so completely different from the one Cat lived in. There was no way her own family problems were as challenging as the poverty and homelessness that Izzie saw in her hometown every day.

Talking to Aidan, though, was different. He didn't offer advice. He didn't point out how irrational her feelings about Boston were, or tell her it should be easy to get used to a new parent in her life. No, he just listened—quietly and thoughtfully, all the while giving her an eagle-eye tour of the forest, too. He used the wildlife checklist in their study guide to label all the different types of plants and animals they saw, and his eyes lit up whenever he spotted something new. They caught sight of quetzal birds with their long, vibrantly colored tails; a jaguar on the prowl for food; and even a couple of sleepy sloths.

As they walked through the canopy, Cat talked about her parents' awful fights and her dad's long absences, about how much she loved Arizona and her old friends. She didn't know how long she went on before she stopped, out of breath and blushing, realizing she was in the middle of spilling her heart to an almost complete stranger.

"Sorry," she said. "I usually talk to Sabrina about this, but lately she's been busy with Brian. You should've told me to shut up."

"Nah. It's tough to be a member of Generation 'Ex.'

You've got to vent about it. Besides," he said with a grin, "it was getting juicy. I was waiting for you to tell me that Ted was your dad's long-lost twin brother seeking revenge."

Cat laughed. "Sorry to disappoint you, but it's not as dramatic as a soap opera."

"At least your parents aren't fighting anymore," Aidan said. "My parents fought all the time when I was a kid. They'd even throw things at each other. Sometimes it got so bad, my dad would sleep at a hotel so he wouldn't have to deal."

"Wow," Cat said. "I guess I got lucky there. My dad was gone so much, even when they fought, it was only for a few days at a time before he left on another trip. What happened with your parents?"

"Eventually, they stopped fighting and did what was best for them…and me," he said. "They figured out what they needed to be happy, and went after it." He shrugged. "Into everyone's family, a little dysfunctionality must fall."

"I guess I should just be grateful my dad doesn't have an evil twin." Cat laughed.

"That you know of," Aidan added. "If one pops up someday, you might just have the makings of a Daytime Emmy."

"Hey, where have you two been?" Pete rounded a corner of the gangplank. "You missed all the excitement. Izzie yelled at Brian for using his flash when he took a picture of a tree frog. The poor little webbed fella's probably *still* seeing stars. And Carlos and Sebastian were getting ready to form a search party for you guys."

"We took a wrong turn at the tree." Aidan laughed.

Cat saw that they'd caught up with the rest of the group, and she was almost sad when Rachel rushed over, followed by Izzie, both chatting excitedly about everything they'd seen. She could've stayed in the forest talking to Aidan for the rest of the day.

Over the course of their walk in the clouds, she'd found a true friend. But as she boarded the bus to head back to Oaxaca, their long talk wasn't what stuck in her mind. What she couldn't shake out of her head, no matter how hard she tried, was the way his hands had wrapped around her waist, pulling her back to safety.

Chapter Six

To: lilmermaid@email.com

From: enginuity@email.com

Happy, HAPPY birthday, Cat! It's hard to believe that seventeen years ago today you came into my life. Your winter break is a long way off, but we'll celebrate your birthday, Halloween, Thanksgiving, Christmas, and all the other holidays I missed when you come out to visit me then. And this year, I promise I'll be in Scottsdale the whole time. The attached photo is of me and the CEO of Enginuity Corp., standing in front of the Sydney Opera House. You'd love Australia, Cat. The water here is beautiful. Someday I'll bring you here and we can swim for hours. Tomorrow I leave for Capetown, but I'll try to call you from there. I sent a birthday present to your mom's in Boston. I love you, sweetie. Happy Birthday!

Love,

Dad

It was only eight o'clock in the morning, but Cat's birthday was already off to a bad start. She'd never been big on birthdays to begin with, and this was an "in-between" one anyway. She already had her driver's license, but she still wasn't old enough to vote, or to drink. Regardless, she'd never had everyone forget her birthday before. Well, almost everyone. Her dad had remembered, so at least that had been something, but it was still bittersweet. Her dad knew better than to forget her birthday these days (he seemed to sense he was on thin ice with her), but how many of her birthdays, not to mention Christmases and Thanskgivings, had he missed because of business over the years? He was always making promises about being home, but most of the time, they'd been empty ones. She'd learned, after being burned one too many times, to take his big plans, and his big birthday wishes, with a grain of salt. She was glad that he'd remembered, but she hoped some-one else would, too. All throughout breakfast that morning,

though, Abril, José, and Izzie had been silent. She couldn't get mad at them. They couldn't possibly have known her birthday was July 18. She could, however, get mad at Sabrina. Not so much as a peep out of her—the girl whom she'd spent every birthday with since she was ten years old!

When Sabrina had arrived at the work site, she'd chatted up a storm with Cat, as usual, but then headed off to help mix some cement with Brian without wishing her a "Happy happy!" Cat's cell phone stayed quiet, too, and she'd thought that for sure her mom would call her. Her mom never would've forgotten her birthday before Ted came along. Cat guessed she was probably off doing some disgustingly romantic thing with Ted today, too busy to remember the birth of her own flesh and blood!

At least she had plenty of work on the orphans' school to keep her busy. In the three weeks since they'd begun the project, progress had been slow. The dimensions of the foundation had just been poured last week, and now the job of putting up the basic framework of the building began. Sebastian and Señor Sanchez were the only ones allowed to work with the wood saw, but the students had been equipped with hammers, nail guns, and work belts. For hours each day, rhythmic hammering sounded from all corners of the site.

Soon, her birthday was long forgotten as Cat became absorbed in her work. She focused on nailing together a line of wood beams that would eventually become part of one of the building's walls. She bent the first few nails, but after Señor Sanchez showed her how to use the gun the right way, she got the hang of it. Sweat soon beaded her face and her shirt, but she didn't stop, even when, in the distance, she heard faint singing.

The singing grew louder, and, finally, Cat glanced up to see Izzie, holding a candlelit cake, and leading everyone else in a slightly off-key version of "Feliz Cumpleaños." Sabrina, Pete, Rachel, and Aidan were right beside her, belting out the song with a theatrical enthusiasm that made Cat giggle.

"How did you know?" Cat asked Izzie as she cut the cake.

"Tus padres," Izzie said, grinning. "My mom said they e-mailed her. They gave her a recipe, too. For this." She nodded to the cake. *"El pastel de queso."*

"Cheesecake!" Cat said. "I can't believe it!" Abril had covered the cake with pink icing, so Cat hadn't recognized her favorite dessert. But once she tasted it, she recognized her mom's recipe…delish. So her mom had sneaked an e-mail to Abril. She'd have to call and thank her.

"Happy birthday!" Sabrina cried, pouncing on her with a hug.

"I thought you forgot," Cat admitted.

"Not a chance," Sabrina said. "Izzie and I plotted the

whole thing yesterday during lunch. We wanted to surprise you." She pulled out a small box wrapped in colorful paper and handed it to her.

"They're beautiful!" Cat cried when she unwrapped a pair of elaborately engraved dangle earrings. Normally, she never wore anything but simple silver studs, but these were a work of art, and, to please Sabrina, she had to at least try them on. She wasn't sure she'd wear them too often, but still, she liked the way they tinkled happily.

"They're an ancient design," Izzie said, admiring them. "See the woman etched on the earrings? She's Ixzaluoh, the Mayan goddess of water."

"How lucky is that? I picked out the perfect ones for you, Cat, and they look fantastic with your short hair!" Sabrina beamed as Cat shook her head, making the earrings dance back and forth against her bare neck.

"Mmmmm, I vant to bite your neck," Pete said with a fake Transylvanian accent.

"Is there anything that doesn't kick your hormones into hyperdrive, Pete?" Rachel asked, slugging him playfully on the shoulder.

"Let me think about that," Pete said. "Um...no."

"Hey, you can't blame Pete for having good taste." Aidan grinned.

"Thanks." Cat blushed, caught off guard by Aidan's bright eyes, looking at her intently, and she quickly slipped the earrings back into the box. "But they're not a good match for this outfit." She motioned to her fatigue-style shorts and Arizona U T-shirt.

"Who cares?" Aidan said. "Any girl who's picture-perfect every day is trying too hard. Besides, birthday girls don't have to match."

He walked away with Pete and Rachel, and Izzie and Sabrina turned toward Cat with huge grins.

"He's got a crush on you," Sabrina singsonged.

"Who? Pete?" Cat rolled her eyes. "He crushes on *everybody.*"

Sabrina and Izzie burst into laughter, and Cat stared at them blankly.

"What's so funny?" she asked.

"Just keep on wearing those earrings, girl," Sabrina said to Cat. "They're your magic charm. And this is only part of your present. The rest you get this afternoon."

"What's this afternoon?" Cat asked.

"The Domingases told me I could have you over to the house for some birthday-girl bonding," Sabrina said. "That's all I'm telling you. The rest of the details are classified."

"Is Brian coming along, too?" Cat asked, grinning. "'Cause I've got to give him credit. If he's into girl bonding, he's one enlightened guy."

"Are you kidding?" Sabrina laughed. "This is a girls-only affair. No boys allowed. Besides, Brian's sitting in on a poli sci class over at Oaxaca University this afternoon. He wants to write a paper on Oaxacan government for extra

credit. He's hoping he might be able to use some of it in his application to Stanford next year."

"Overachiever," Cat said.

"Look who's talking," Sabrina teased. "No matter how hard you try to sabotage your grades, you're still a straight-A student at heart."

"Careful, you'll blow my cover," Cat said. "If my parents find out I was faking my bad grades in Boston, I'll never be able to get so much as a B again."

"You won't last the summer," Sabrina said, smiling. "Your grades are going up as we speak."

It was true. In fact, Sebastian had returned her folk-art and cloud-forest papers yesterday with grades of B. They were the first grades above a C she'd gotten since she'd tried (but failed) to flunk in Boston. The B's secretly felt good, but she wasn't about to tell that to her mom or Ted. They wouldn't see her grades until the end of the semester, and Cat was enjoying writing her program papers, now that they were going more smoothly. Little by little, she was remembering how to spell Spanish words. And *speaking* Spanish was second nature to her now. She loved stringing the words together in conversation—it was like a form of poetry. She almost never spoke English anymore, unless she had to. Of course, she still used Izzie as her fallback Spanish/English dictionary when she forgot how to spell a word in one of her essays, but she was making progress.

"You know, I'm not the only one who has a little overachiever in me," Cat said to Sabrina. "I'm surprised you don't want to go along with Brian to hear the lecture, Ms. Student Body President."

"You know I don't believe in textbook politics." Sabrina grinned. "I prefer direct contact with the people."

"So, it'll just be you and me this afternoon?" Cat asked. Sabrina nodded. "You and me."

Cat smiled. Hearing that was the best birthday present she could've gotten.

Sabrina stuck to her word, and, a few hours later, the two of them were sprawled out on the couch in the Domingases' living room, a bowl of roasted blue pumpkin seeds (aka Mexican popcorn) between them. Cat had just kicked off her shoes and curled up into a comfy position when Sabrina pulled two videos out of her backpack. Cat recognized Molly Ringwald's face on them instantly, underneath the titles *Dieciseis Velas* and *La Chica de Rosa*.

"I don't believe it," Cat said. "*Sixteen Candles* and *Pretty in Pink*...in Spanish! I didn't even know they made dubbed versions of these."

"Maria took me to a movie rental place right off the *zócalo*, and there they were." Sabrina grinned. "Since we won't be together for midterms this fall, I figured we could have our movie marathon a little early. Although we really should call it *Seventeen Candles*, in honor of today."

"Thanks, Sabrina." Cat smiled. "This is an amazing gift.

Who knew that John Hughes movies had global fans?"

"Well, I looked for your favorite, *Some Kind of Wonderful*," Sabrina said, popping one of the videos into the Domingases' VCR. "But no joy. I really wanted to rent that one. It's so fitting. You and Aidan totally have the whole best-friend-turns-boyfriend story line going on."

Cat nearly choked on a pumpkin seed. "What are you talking about? We're just friends."

"Please. Did you see the way he was looking at you this morning? Like you were the only girl in the world." Sabrina smiled.

"Yeah, right. He was looking at me like I was a girl who needed a serious shower." Cat laughed. "I'm sure I made a real pretty picture—in my work boots, holding a nail gun, with sweat running down my face."

"Why do you always find it so hard to believe that a guy might be interested in you? Some guys think women wielding tools are hot." Sabrina grinned. "Face it, Cat. He's into you."

Cat took a deep breath, trying to calm her fluttering heart. She'd always related to Watts, the blond tomboy in *Some Kind of Wonderful*, but that didn't mean she wanted to fall for her guy pal the way Watts had. "Aidan doesn't like me," she protested. "I don't *want* him to like me."

Sabrina looked at Cat, suddenly serious. "Come on. I've watched you talking to him at the work site. And Bri told me that you and Aidan did the cloud-forest walk with each other, and I saw your smile when you got on the bus afterward. Are you sure you don't want this, too?"

"I'm positive," Cat said. "It would just complicate things, not to mention screw up our friendship." Then she quickly changed subjects. "Now, speaking of Brian, how are things going with you two? Has he said the big L-word yet?"

Just as Cat hoped, Sabrina immediately launched into a glowing ode to Brian, and the heat was off of her, at least for the time being. But as they watched Molly Ringwald's brave romance and social disasters for the next few hours, Aidan's face kept flashing before Cat's eyes. The harder she tried to push it away, the longer it stayed. And there wasn't a single thing she could do about it.

Later that night, completely stuffed from an amazing birthday dinner of *frijoles* and tamales that Abril and José had cooked for her, Cat sat down in the Canuls' courtyard and dialed her mom's number on her cell. While she'd been watching movies with Sabrina, her mom and Ted had left her a message, singing a rendition of "Happy Birthday" that sounded more like dogs howling than actual music. This was the first chance she'd had to return their call.

"Hi, Mom," Cat said when her mother picked up.

"My birthday girl!" her mom said. "Did you get our message?"

"Yes." Cat laughed. "I had to hold the phone a foot away to keep my eardrums from exploding."

"Hey, don't make fun of your tone-deaf mother."

"Okay, okay," Cat said. "Thanks for giving Abril that cheesecake recipe. What a great surprise."

"I'm so glad she made it for you!" her mom said. "But it wasn't my idea to send the recipe."

"It wasn't?" Cat said. "But Izzie told me you e-mailed it."

"I did," her mom said, "but it was Ted's idea. I told him that I felt bad you weren't going to get your favorite dessert for your birthday this year. He's the one who suggested e-mailing it to the Canuls. He's such a sweetheart."

"Oh," Cat said. This was the last thing she'd expected to hear. "Well, um"—she struggled with what she was about to say—"tell him I said thank you."

"Do you want to tell him yourself? He just got home from work."

"No!" Cat said, panicking. Talk about awkward. "No," she said, a little less adamantly this time. "I have an essay to write, so I should go."

"Okay," her mom said. "Say hello to the Canuls for us. And happy birthday again, honey."

"Thanks, Mom," Cat said. "Good night."

After she hung up, Cat headed for Izzie's room to put the questions racing through her head down in her journal:

July 18, 9:30 P.M.

Seventeen is off to a confusing start. Maybe it's

Aidan's love for swimming. Or how he talks to me about my family...like he really gets them, and me. I don't know...there's something about him that sucks the air right out of me. Argh! But Sabrina's wrong about him liking me. I wish she'd never said anything about it. And now Ted's being nice to me and messing things up, too. Is he trying to bribe me into liking him? Or is he just being nice to make Mom happy? I wanted to go away this summer to try to simplify my life, but instead, things are more complicated than ever.

Note to Self: All stepparents—correction—all stepparents and <u>all boys</u> should come with owners' manuals for figuring them out.

Cat had hoped that with midterms less than a week away, she'd at least get a break from the rest of her worries. But no such luck. As everyone got serious about studying over their lunch break at the site the next day, Cat tried to focus on the list of topics Sebastian had given them on the exam material. But thoughts about Aidan kept running through her head at the most inconvenient times. Like earlier today, when he'd smiled at her from the ladder where he stood putting shingles on the school's roof. Or just a few minutes

ago when he'd ruffled her hair playfully right before he collapsed under the tree for a break. Why was it that now that Sabrina had pointed out the possibility of his being interested in her, Cat was so aware of every look he gave her?

She flipped the pages of her study guide, trying in vain to focus on the quiz Rachel was giving her and Pete.

"It's too hot to think," she moaned. This was one of the hottest days of the summer so far. Sabrina and Brian were taking catnaps in the grass a few feet away, and the rest of the group was dropping like flies, too, collapsing in the shade to escape the brutal sun. Cat had brought a wheelbarrow of cement with her to the trees, so at least she could try to stay productive and mix it while she cooled off. But so far, she was failing at the mixing and the cooling off.

"Just two more questions," Rachel prodded. "We still haven't reviewed the test-prep questions in the rain forest and nature science section of the study guide."

"Our brains are fried," Pete griped pathetically. "I quit."

"Me, too," Cat seconded. "No more studying." She looked out at the work site, where Izzie, Sebastian, and the other advisers were still out in the full sun, layering the framework of the school with sheets of drywall. "I just don't get how she does it," she said, nodding toward Izzie. "She's unstoppable."

"Or insane," Rachel said.

"I wish we were building a pool." Cat wiped her brow. "We'd put it to good use."

Pete flopped back in the grass near Aidan. "You ladies all in bikinis, playing in the water." He closed his eyes and grinned. "I'm liking this picture."

"Just keep on dreaming, Petey," Cat said. "Anyway, I thought you had your heart set on your Spanish lady?"

"Oh, I do," Pete said. "But if, by some tragic twist of fate, she can't be found, who will be the great Don Juan's paramour?" He winked at her with hilariously bad form.

"It's a tempting offer," Cat said, laughing. "But I'm a lost cause. I'm a romantically challenged individual...totally dating impaired."

"Tragic," Pete said. "I guess I'll go see if Izzie's interested. But for the record, you were my first choice." He and Rachel headed toward the half-finished school building, leaving Cat and Aidan alone.

"So, what's this dating-impaired thing all about?" Aidan asked her. "I mean, hypothetically speaking, of course, if a very nice guy who thinks you're a very cool girl happened to come along and ask you out on a date, what would you do?"

"I'd tell him thanks, but no thanks," Cat said. "It doesn't matter, though, guys never ask me out. They're too busy forgetting I'm a girl."

"But say one *did* ask you out," Aidan said. "Would you still say no, even if he was incredibly handsome and totally irresistible?"

Cat laughed. "Well, I'd have to know more about this

hypothetical guy before making a decision," she said, humoring him. "For instance, what's he look like?"

"Well, to say he's incredibly handsome might be a slight exaggeration," Aidan said, "but hopefully you'd find him irresistible. Let's say he's got brown hair and green eyes. He's about five-eleven, if he's being totally honest and not adding an extra inch."

"Sounds cute," Cat said, absently stirring the cement in the wheelbarrow. "But looks aren't that important to me. He'd have to know me pretty well."

"Oh, he does," Aidan said. "He knows you hate Boston, but you love cheesecake. You tug on that short piece of hair right above your left ear whenever you're nervous. And you smile whenever you talk about Arizona."

Cat froze, quickly pulling her hand from her head, where she'd been tugging on her hair. She hadn't even realized she'd been doing that. And why was her heart suddenly flopping? She'd thought this was just some good-natured teasing, but she wasn't so sure anymore.

"Since I don't know anybody who fits that description, this is a hypothetical impossibility." She attempted a light laugh, hoping to end the conversation.

"Actually, you do," Aidan said with a shy smile. "Me."

Cat dropped her eyes from his, blushing furiously, at a loss for words. She could sense his eyes on her as he waited for a response.

"Um, I should really go find Izzie," Cat mumbled. "I

promised to help her finish that drywall." She hurriedly lifted the wheelbarrow, but lost her grip, and it tipped sideways, spilling all of the wet cement onto the grass.

Sebastian rushed over from the field and began shoveling what he could salvage of the cement back into the wheelbarrow.

"It broke in the fall," Cat said, pointing to the splintered wheelbarrow handle. "I'm sorry."

Sebastian inspected it. "Don't worry," he said. "I think it's fixable."

Cat glanced up to find Aidan still looking at her, and, suddenly, she couldn't breathe. "I have to go," she said. "Izzie..." Her voice died as she rushed away.

"¿Qué pasó?" Izzie asked when she saw Cat coming toward her. "You look like you've just seen La Llorona."

"Worse than that," Cat moaned. Izzie had told her about La Llorona, the ghost of the weeping woman from Mexican folklore. Every time the wind howled at night at the Canuls', Abril blamed La Llorona. "I can handle a depressed ghost over guy trouble any day."

Izzie laughed. "So Pete asked you out, too?"

That brought a weak smile to Cat's face, and she nodded. "But so did Aidan," she said miserably.

"¡Finalmente!" Izzie said. "He took long enough to do it."

"What?" Cat gaped at her.

"Don't tell me you're surprised," Izzie said. "Everyone knows he likes you."

"But I'm emotionally unavailable," Cat cried. "Isn't it obvious? The one and only time a guy thinks of me as more than a friend, and I totally freak. Point proven." She tugged at her hair. "Why do guys have to be so confusing?"

"If I knew the answer to that one," Izzie said, "I'd make enough money to find every one of my orphans a family. So how did you answer Aidan?"

"I didn't," Cat mumbled.

"¿Por qué?" Izzie asked.

"Because...I ran away," Cat said. Even as the words left her mouth, she realized how ridiculous they sounded.

Izzie stared at her, and they both started laughing.

"You know, one of my country's great revolutionaries, Emiliano Zapata, had a saying," Izzie said. *"Prefiero morir de pie que vivir siempre de rodillas."*

"It's better to die on your feet than live on your knees?" Cat laughed. "So, dating *could* potentially kill me, and this is a good thing...why?"

"You're missing the point." Izzie rolled her eyes. "Life would be boring without a little risk. Revolutionaries risked their lives for freedom. You can risk your heart."

"My mom tried that with my dad," Cat said. "And so did I. It didn't work out too well for either one of us. There's no way I'm letting that happen to me again."

"Stubborn girl!" Izzie sighed, then grinned mischievously. "But you can't run from Aidan forever."

And she was right. Even though Cat tried her best to

avoid Aidan for the rest of the day, he cornered her a few hours later when she was taking a water break.

"You know, I've been turned down before," Aidan said with a grin. "But I've never had a girl run away. That's a new experience for me."

Cat couldn't help smiling, and some of her panic subsided. "Sorry about that."

"It's a good thing I have such a healthy ego." Aidan laughed. "I think I'll live. But you never answered me."

Cat let out a small sigh. Their friendship had started off so great, and now it was going to fall apart completely. "I can't, Aidan. I'm not up for dating right now. Not with everything that's happened the past couple years with my dad and my family. I just need some time to...adjust." She gave him a smile. "Besides, I'm much better at being friends with guys than dating them."

"You never know. You might be better at dating than you think."

"Maybe so, but I don't think nearly hyperventilating at the idea of a date is a particularly promising sign." Cat laughed. "And you're such an amazing friend, I don't want to risk it. But do you think we can still hang out together? I'd really like that."

"I don't know," he said with mock seriousness. "I'll have to check my calendar, because I've got a couple of really hot dates lined up for this week. And, you know, having a girl 'friend' might seriously cramp my style..."

"Aidan!" Cat said, elbowing him.

He broke into laughter. "Sure. We can still hang out."

He started to leave, but Cat stopped him. "Hey, thanks for understanding."

Aidan smiled. "That's what friends are for, right?"

Cat let out a relieved breath as he walked away. But that night, as she got ready for bed, she felt anything but relieved. She pulled out her journal and began writing:

July 19, 8:00 P.M.

What is wrong with me????? I am definitely NOT interested in Aidan. So...why can't I stop thinking about him? Yes, I've noticed how on hot days like today, his hair sticks to his forehead in a very cute way, with little bits of it curling up around his ears. And yes, I've seen how his eyes turn a lighter shade of green in the sunlight. But no, I'm NOT going to do a single thing about it, except fight like hell not to think about it.

Note to Self: It's always better to have guys as friends than as boyfriends. More fun, less heartache. (Remind yourself of this at least three times daily, especially when you see Aidan.)

Chapter Seven

Cat stared up at the cloudless sky as she floated on her back in the warm water, beaming. This was heaven. The Parque Nacional Agua Azul was a huge nature park made up of pool after pool of aqua waters, with countless sparkling waterfalls spilling into each one. Nothing in the States even came close to this. The water was beautiful, cool, and refreshing, and everyone was enjoying it. Aidan, Pete, Amber, and Rachel were having chicken fights at the far end of the pool. Sabrina was lounging on a rock in the sun, and Brian, Jimmy, and Rob were leaping from the top of the twenty-foot waterfall pouring into the pool.

Cat flipped over and swam toward Izzie, who was standing underneath one of the smaller waterfalls, letting it douse her hair. "Now this is my kind of eco-education," Cat said. "If we hadn't gotten off that bus soon, I was going to hurt someone."

"*Yo también.*" Izzie nodded in agreement. "*Especialmente con el cantando de Pete.* Especially with Pete's singing. What was that awful song?"

"'You've Lost That Lovin' Feeling.' " Cat grinned at Izzie's scowl. "Oh, come on, Izzie, he was trying to seduce you with music."

"Kill me is more like it." Izzie shuddered.

Cat laughed as she remembered how Pete's rendition of the song had sounded more like a cat's yowl than anything close to sexy. But after seven hours being cooped up on the un-air-conditioned program bus, who could blame the guy for going a little stir-crazy? They'd left Oaxaca two days ago for a five-day/four-night eco-educational tour to Palenque, the largest archaeological site for ancient Mayan ruins close to the city. But as Cat had discovered during the painfully long bus ride, "close" actually meant a fifteen-hour drive, and, so far, they had made it only three-quarters of the way there. There was no chance of taking trains, since there were none that ran through this part of Mexico, and flying wasn't in the semester budget. Driving was the only option.

Sebastian had broken the trip up with stops at Monte

Albán, the best-preserved ancient Zapotec city near Oaxaca; Mexico's version of the Grand Canyon, called Cañón del Sumidero; and the tiny colonial town of San Crístobal de las Casas. Their next program essay would be on ancient archaeological sights, so everyone tried their best to concentrate and take careful notes. But, still, each stop took only a couple hours out of a very long, very hot ride. The bus had traversed everything from smooth, relatively well-kept highways to dusty dirt roads, and Cat had a new appreciation for how easy it was to travel in the States. In southern Mexico, transportation wasn't simple or easy, and by today, everyone had gotten a bit fed up, which was why they'd taken this detour to Agua Azul.

"Well, there was one big plus to Pete's nonstop singing," Cat told Izzie as she splashed some water through her hair. "If it weren't for him, Sebastian might never have gotten that migraine and agreed to stop here. And, after those midterms on Tuesday, I'm in serious need of this R and R." When Sebastian and Señor Mendoza, Aidan's host dad and the guest lecturer for this trip, had called for an emergency "restorative" stop at the park, they were both looking harried. Then again, Sebastian had been trying to grade the midterms on a bus filled with semi-hysterical students. That could give anyone a headache.

"I still don't know why you worried so much about that test," Izzie said. "You speak Spanish better than I do now. And your writing's gotten better."

"We'll see how much better when I get the grade," Cat said, but she knew from the good feeling she'd gotten after the test that she'd done well. She'd aced the oral exam, where she'd had to describe three places of cultural significance they'd studied on eco-tours so far this semester. She'd come to love Mexico so much that it was easy for her to talk about the cloud forest, the museums, and the other things she'd seen. Even the written portion of the test hadn't been that bad. Thanks to Izzie and her passion for revolutionaries, she knew more about Benito Juárez and the Mexican Revolution than she'd ever thought possible. Izzie had quizzed her on spelling last week to prep, too, and Cat had stumbled only a few times during the test.

"At least now that it's over," Izzie said, "everyone can focus on the orphan school. There's so much left to do. I don't know how we're going to finish it all."

"We will," Cat said. "We're making progress." And they were. The walls were up, the roof was finished, and this week electricity and plumbing had been put into the building. Pete's host dad, Señor Hernandez, was an electrician, and Rachel's host family, the Vegases, had three sons who ran a plumbing business. It took almost the entire week for everyone to dig a water-line system to an underground well they'd put in. The bathroom fixtures and overhead lights still had to be installed, and tile floors had to be laid down in most of the classrooms. That would be their task for next week. But right now, with the sun shining down and the cool water surrounding them, next week felt like it was ages away.

"Hey! Come on, you guys!" Aidan called from where he and Pete were waging a splashing war against Rachel toward the deeper end of the pool. "Amber quit, and we need more victims—I mean, players—for chicken fights."

"Come on, ladies." Pete grinned. "I know you're just dying to feel my biceps."

"Please," Rachel begged Cat, looking seriously water-logged. "They show no mercy. Save me."

"We'll play," Cat said, swimming over with Izzie. "But only on one condition. No singing allowed."

"Bummer," Aidan said. "We had a duet of 'Unchained Melody' all lined up."

"You're starting, too?" Cat said. "Please...don't encourage Pete."

"Musical genius is so often misunderstood," Pete said forlornly, just before Izzie dunked him.

Aidan grinned mischievously at Cat.

"Oh no," Cat said, backing away. "Don't even think ab—" A huge wave of water splashed over her, going up her nose in the process. She wiped her eyes and laughed. "You're a dead man," she said, lunging at him.

"You've got to catch me first," he teased.

Cat grinned as she dunked him, thankful that her friendship with Aidan hadn't changed, even with the talk they'd had about dating. Aidan seemed happy spending

time with her, and, after she got over her initial freak-out, she had been able to relax around him again, too. Keeping things on the platonic level had been a good call. At least…that's what she told herself five hundred times a day.

Three rounds of chicken fights later, Cat and Aidan were about to declare victory (Pete wasn't much of a match, since he was roughly half the size of everyone else, girls included), when she heard Sabrina calling her.

She looked up to see Sabrina standing with Brian at the top of the twenty-foot waterfall.

"Cat!" Sabrina waved. "Come on up!"

Cat stared in disbelief. What was Sabrina *doing* up there? She could see Sabrina's chattering teeth and shaking knees even from where she was, and it was close to ninety degrees out, so there was no way she was shaking from cold. Sabrina was terrified, but she was trying her best to hide it from Brian, giving him a loving smile, albeit nervously. Of course, only Cat knew her well enough to catch on. She sighed. Well, she certainly wasn't going to let Sabrina faint up there. If she left it up to Brian, he'd be too busy gabbing with Jimmy and Rob to catch her. She pulled herself out of the pool and climbed up the steep, slippery path to the top of the falls.

"What are you doing?" she asked them when she reached the top.

"Having some fun," Brian said, laughing. "This is a

choice jump." He wrapped his arms around Sabrina's waist. "Come on, sweets, give it a try."

"Okay." Sabrina giggled wildly, sounding like she was bordering on hysteria. She looked at Cat with pleading eyes, and then back at Brian. Cat could almost see the wheels turning. Sabrina wanted so much to please Brian, but she was petrified.

"Sabrina—" Cat started.

"No," Sabrina interrupted. "I want to."

"Okay," Cat said. "We'll do it together. We'll count to three, run, and jump. Don't think...just do it."

Sabrina nodded, and Cat guessed she was too scared to utter one word. They moved closer to the edge, standing side by side.

"One," Cat started. "Two." She poised her body, ready to run. "Three!"

She took off, knowing that Sabrina would stay frozen unless she saw her move first. Out of the corner of her eye, Cat saw Sabrina catch up to her, and then they were both airborne.

Cat didn't hear Sabrina scream bloody murder, like Brian said she did afterward. She heard the warm air rushing past her. She saw the blue sky above her and bluer water below her as her toes pointed and her body curled naturally into a twisting dive.

She shot straight into the pool, feeling only the tiniest

splash rise up over her toes as the silent water world engulfed her. She touched the bottom of the pool, pushed off, and broke through the surface, laughing.

For a second, everyone stared at her in absolute silence. Izzie was the first one to break it. *"¡Fantástico!"* she cried.

"I can't believe I missed most of that!" Sabrina hugged her. "I saw you hit the water, though. Not even a ripple. Just like in Arizona. A perfect ten!"

"Impressive, Cat!" Brian called down from the top of the waterfall.

Pete and Rachel clapped and hooted. "Aerodynamic and swimsuit-clad," Pete said admiringly. "Marry me?"

"Pete!" everyone yelled at once.

"Sorry, sorry," Pete said sheepishly. "But a guy can dream, can't he?"

After the excitement died down a bit, Aidan swam over to Cat. "Just when I thought I had you all figured out, you go and pull an Olympic-worthy stunt." He grinned. "Where did you learn to do a forward-flying somersault pike? And don't tell me you just winged it. Nobody wings that dive."

Cat shrugged, wanting to downplay it. Her arms and legs were still tingling with adrenaline. She'd forgotten how much she loved that rush—the feel of all her muscles working as a unit, the way the water swallowed her up with a neat little hiccup if she got the dive perfect. She almost wished she hadn't made the dive, though, because now she felt beyond any doubt how much she really missed it.

"I was in the Scottsdale Diving Club in Arizona, on the junior national circuit," Cat said quietly. "But I'm out of practice. I haven't dived since we moved."

She got out of the water and lay down on her towel to dry off, hoping that would be the end of the conversation. But Aidan sat down on the rock beside her.

"Why not?" he asked, persisting. "North Harbor has an awesome club and varsity team."

Cat threw up her hands in frustration. She didn't want to deal with making explanations, especially not to Aidan, who always seemed to see right through her. "Because I didn't feel like it, okay?" she finally said. "I hate that my mom and Ted made me move. I hate that I lost all my friends from Scottsdale except for Sabrina. Diving would never be the same in Boston as it was in Arizona." She frowned. "It doesn't matter anyway, so can we drop it?"

"Hey, don't get so defensive," Aidan said. "It was just a question." He smiled.

"Sorry." Cat sighed. "I just don't feel like talking about it. That dive back there was a mistake...I don't know what I was thinking..."

"Maybe you weren't thinking," Aidan said, "and that's why it happened. It's pretty cool that you're so comfortable with diving that it's automatic like that. I get that feeling when I'm swimming, too. I panic right before I push off the block into the pool, but once I hit the water, my body goes on autopilot. And the next thing I know, my fingers touch

the wall, and I'm pulling myself out of the water after a fifty-meter relay, wondering how the heck I did it." He grinned. "You can't beat that high. You must really miss it."

"No!" Cat said, louder and more adamantly than she'd meant to. "I mean, not really," she said, more quietly this time. "I don't."

"Okay, whatever you say." He shrugged. "But for the record, I don't think anyone could dive like that without loving every second of it." He watched her, waiting, but when minutes passed and she still said nothing, he stood up to go. "Is it your mom and Ted," he said quietly, "or *you* who's going to regret it the most if you quit for good?"

She'd been dreading that question. She'd known it was coming, and now she was dreading even more how to answer it. So she didn't. She waited until he was a safe distance away before she flopped back on her towel in defeat. Why did he always have to be so...so...right all the time? It was enough to make her crazy. And she didn't want to think about the question he'd asked her. But as she gathered her things to head back to the bus, like it or not, that was all she *could* think about.

The next morning, as the sun was barely creeping over the hills, they arrived at Palenque, getting there early to have the whole day to explore. The moment she walked into the mysterious world of ruins, Cat knew this whole trip, and the three days of driving leading up to it, had been worth it.

There was a dampness in the air, even though it was already warm, and fog curled around the edges of the ancient Mayan buildings in an almost spooky way.

"As you can see," Sebastian said, "Palenque is surrounded by dense jungle. But some of these lush hillsides aren't hills at all. They're actually ruins, completely covered by jungle where nature has reclaimed the land. Archaeologists are slowly uncovering some of these buried buildings, and Señor Mendoza himself spent years doing extensive work on this site before his retirement."

Señor Mendoza, Aidan's host dad and the guest lecturer, looked like he had once been an adventurer with his rumpled white hair and weathered face. Cat remembered that Aidan had mentioned once how he'd traveled through most of Central America to research the ruins, and the way his crinkled old eyes glowed as he gave them the history of Palenque showed how passionate he was about archaeology.

He walked the group around to each of the buildings that had already been excavated. The palace was the largest of the ruins, standing in the center of the site on a platform surrounded by crumbling courtyards and long corridors of rooms. At one end of it a four-story tower, reaching toward the sky, stood guard.

"This tower," Señor Mendoza said, "was most likely used as an observatory. The ancient Maya had a very advanced knowledge of astronomy. They followed the

movements of the stars and planets, and they even calculated the orbit of Venus with amazing accuracy, without the use of telescopes, clocks, or space travel."

From there, he went on to show them the Temple of Inscriptions and the Temple of the Sun, two smaller buildings with pyramid-style construction. The steps leading up the Temple of the Sun were tall and hard to climb, but the view from the top of the surrounding jungle was breathtaking. Cat wondered at what a feat of engineering it must have taken to build such stately stone pyramids before 100 B.C.

"For many years," Señor Mendoza explained, "archaeologists believed that the Maya were a peaceful people who didn't partake in the warfare or human sacrifice so common to other Mesoamerican civilizations. But recently, we've discovered that they performed bloodletting and sacrificial rituals on their captives. Can anyone guess why?"

"Too much TV violence?" Brian kidded.

"Cannibalism?" Sabrina guessed.

"It wasn't a thirst for blood." Cat spoke up. "It was an attempt to maintain balance. The Mayans believed that death was a means of renewing life in nature." Izzie had explained the whole ritual to her during their never-ending bus ride.

"*Gracias*, Cat. *Perfecto*," Señor Mendoza said. "In nature, the death of leaves and flowers in the fall brings about new growth in the spring. So the Mayans believed that offerings of death would result in new births and the continuation of their people."

"It's still twisted, if you ask me," Brian muttered.

"We didn't," Izzie answered, to which Aidan and Cat burst out laughing.

It felt good to laugh with Aidan, sort of like an ice-breaker. Cat had been avoiding one-on-one time with him since yesterday afternoon at Agua Azul. She wasn't mad at him, she just didn't like feeling so off balance around him. It was like he could map out all of her fears about Boston, about diving, about dating, and put them into words, even when she couldn't. It was infuriating, but also kind of...sexy? Part of her liked that he got her so well. But it was terrifying, too. And the last thing she wanted was for him to find how she felt.

She focused on studying Palenque instead, taking in the eerie silence and magic of the temples. While Izzie left her to get their sack lunches from the bus, Cat wandered into the Temple of Inscriptions. She wanted to get a closer look at the elaborate glyphs carved into the walls. She sat down on a bench in a room where the sarcophagus of one of the Mayan royalty was kept, trying to describe everything that she saw in her study-guide notes. She'd already taken tons of photographs, too, but she knew she'd never be able to truly capture the strange, otherworldly feel of this place on paper or film.

"In the mood for company?" a voice asked, making her

jump, and she turned to see Aidan standing in the door-way.

"I've already got some," she said jokingly, pointing to the sarcophagus.

Aidan smiled. "Somehow, I don't think he's the most lively conversationalist."

Cat laughed nervously, trying to calm her racing heart. This was just great. She was here...alone...with Aidan. This was exactly what she'd been trying to avoid.

"I'm sorry about yesterday," Aidan started. "I wouldn't blame you if you were still mad at me. I shouldn't have asked so many questions about the diving. It's none of my business."

"I'm sorry, too. I lost my temper," she said. "And I'm not really mad. I guess a little bit of truth never hurt anybody." She grinned. "You are stubborn, though."

"Very," Aidan said. "But my charm makes up for that. And stubbornness has its benefits, too. It helps me get what I want."

"Oh, really?" Cat laughed.

He nodded. "And when I mix charm with stubbornness, I have even better results. For instance, if I asked you out again, you might possibly say yes?"

Cat flushed. "I can't," she said, sighing. "I'm sorry, but like I said before, I'm not interested in dating."

"But this wouldn't be a date."

"It wouldn't?" she asked doubtfully.

"No." He shook his head. "It would be hanging out between two friends. No pressure, no expectations, no romance under any circumstances." He grinned. "But no other friends along either. I guess it would be more like... a not-date."

"A not-date?" Cat laughed. "That's a new one. I've never been on a not-date before."

"Then you have to say yes," Aidan said. "You can't knock it 'til you've tried it. And you're not-diving, so why not try not-dating?"

Cat paused. She wanted to be strong. She wanted to be stubborn. She wanted to say no. But when she opened her mouth, what came out was a simple, "Yes."

"Told you." His eyes twinkled. "Charm and stubbornness. The perfect combo."

He stepped out the doorway of the temple just as Izzie stepped inside.

"Did he just ask you out again?" Izzie said.

"Yes...no!" Cat sighed. "Sort of."

"Please tell me you said yes this time," Izzie said, handing Cat her lunch.

"He almost gave up on you, but I told him, *'Una vez más.'* " She smiled.

"Since when are you playing cupid?" Cat gave her a halfhearted glare.

"Coopit? This is an American word?" Izzie asked. "*¿Quién es* 'coopit'?"

"A Hallmark hellion with wings," Cat said, and then added, when she saw Izzie's blank stare. *"Una casamentera con alas.* A matchmaker with wings."

Izzie laughed. "I don't have wings, but somebody has to help you with this."

"I'm not sure this is going to work," Cat said. "Nothing good comes of relationships. Somebody always ends up getting hurt."

"Like your dad hurt you?" Izzie asked.

"Something like that," Cat muttered. "Every time he promised my mom to make more time for us, he promised me, too. But then...nothing."

Izzie patted Cat's shoulder. *"No hagas las cosas más complicadas de las que son en realidad,"* Izzie said. "Don't make things more complicated than they really are. Aidan's not your dad. And you're not marrying him, you're just spending a few hours with him. If your mom had the courage to date again, then you don't have any excuses."

Cat started to protest, and then thought better of it. Even though the whole idea of a "not-date" seemed too hilarious to actually work, she didn't have the energy to keep Aidan at a distance anymore. And more than that, she wasn't sure she wanted to.

Chapter Eight

July 31, 10:44 A.M.

Okay. I'm calm. I'm collected. I still have four hours, fifteen minutes, and forty-two seconds before I meet Aidan. Four hours, fifteen minutes, and forty-two—no, forty-seconds to hyperventilate. I just know I'm going to blow our whole friendship. I love talking to him about his swimming, but isn't that kind of—sporty—to talk about on a date, er, not-date? Maybe I'm supposed to

flirt instead? Oh God—I don't know how to flirt! That's Sabrina's department. Just thinking about it makes my hands sweat—gross! He's going to be repulsed by me! Or, what if, by some miracle, he's not repulsed, and then I start to like him, and he dumps me cold? Wait—he can't dump me because this isn't a real date. Or is dumping allowed on not-dates? Help! This is a big mistake. HUGE.

Cat knew the not-date was supposed to be no-pressure, but, as she dressed on Monday afternoon, she worried about what the rest of this day would bring. Sure, Aidan had said he'd pick her up around three P.M., because in the daylight there'd be less chance for romance. And sure, he'd said they'd go dutch on dinner, if they decided that dinner was even acceptable on a not-date.

"Since we're both new to this not-dating thing, we'll just make up the rules as we go along," he'd teased.

But even though she appreciated his keeping the mood light, she still found herself stressing over her hair and her outfit. And Sabrina wasn't helping, since from the minute she'd found out about the not-date, she'd talked about nothing else.

"It's a step in the right direction," she'd told Cat.

"It's going to be a disaster," Cat told her.

"Only if you panic," Sabrina said. "And I'll make sure you won't."

So now, while Cat dressed, Sabrina and Izzie were on panic patrol. "If we're not here to stop you," Sabrina had teased, "you could make for the hills." It was so close to the truth, Cat couldn't even laugh about it. To make things worse, Izzie and Sabrina were obsessively offering advice, adding to her pre-not-date anxiety.

"I could lend you a skirt to wear," Izzie suggested as she watched Cat rummaging through her side of the closet.

"No way!" Cat cried. "I'd *never* wear a skirt just to go out with a friend."

"What about the earrings I bought you?" Sabrina asked.

Cat took them off the dresser and held them up to her ears. She debated for a few seconds, and then slipped them on. "The earrings, yes. The skirt, no."

"I still don't get why Aidan wanted me to meet him at your parents' gallery," Cat said to Izzie as she pulled on her nice pair of black silk cargo capris and a sea-green top that she'd bought at the Mercado de Abastos last week. "I know he wanted to introduce himself to Abril and José before he took me out. But it's not like this is a real date, so does it really matter?"

"*Él es un caballero verdadero,*" Izzie said.

Sabrina nodded in agreement. "A true gentleman always meets the parents first."

"Did Brian?" Cat said.

"You know the answer to that." Sabrina laughed. "If you were a guy, would *you* want to face my father, the retired Marine colonel? The man who says the number-one rule for dating his daughters is: Don't."

Cat laughed. "Okay, I'll give you that one." If there was a reason for Sabrina's boy craziness, Cat could pretty much pin it on her father, who had forbidden her to date until she was—no, not sixteen—but *sixty*.

She stepped into her simple sandals and turned around to face Sabrina and Izzie. "How do I look?"

"Like you're going to hang out with a friend," Sabrina said. She and Izzie smiled in approval. "The key is not to panic. Have fun. Remember... it's only Aidan."

"Got it." Cat nodded, taking a deep breath. "I can do this."

There was no way she could do this. She was standing in front of the Canuls' gallery, pacing on the sidewalk. She'd just peeked in the window and seen Aidan smiling and chatting away with Abril and José, and now she'd completely frozen up. She couldn't bring herself to step inside, but she couldn't ditch him either. She glanced up again and there was Aidan standing on the sidewalk, blocking her escape route.

"You look like you're about to run for the border." He grinned.

His grin was contagious, and Cat smiled, ignoring her urge to hyperventilate. "The thought crossed my mind."

"Quick, let's go before it happens again," Aidan said.

"But, don't they want me to go inside?" Cat started, confused. Abril and José were waving from the window.

Aidan shook his head. "They've already decided that you're perfectly safe with me." He pulled a car key out of his pocket. "They also agreed to let me use this."

"*I've* never even driven their Jeep before, and they're letting *you*?" Cat said in disbelief. "That's so nice. They are way more laid-back than my parents would be."

"It's just for tonight." Aidan grinned. "I guess they like me. Plus, Izzie put in a good word for me. The bribery helped a lot, too. I told them my parents might be interested in buying a piece of folk art from them."

"You lied?" Cat cried.

"Of course not!" Aidan said. "My parents collect international art. It's their hobby."

"Oh." Cat gave a relieved smile. "So Abril and José are really okay with this?"

Aidan nodded. "And they told me to tell you not to worry, and to have a great time. So, are you ready for our first activity of the day?"

"That all depends on what it involves," Cat said.

"Virgin sacrifices, hallucinogenic mushrooms, and hedonistic dancing." He grinned.

"Sounds perfectly safe." Cat laughed. "Let's go."

"I didn't think you were serious!" Cat cried. They'd taken

the Jeep up to a huge amphitheater set atop the Cerro del Fortín hill overlooking Oaxaca, and now they were waiting in line to get inside for the Guelaguetza show, something Cat had never heard of before, until she started reading the brochure Aidan had just handed her.

"Don't worry," Aidan said, grinning. "They haven't sacrificed any virgins for centuries, and they nixed the mushrooms, too. All those old traditions were replaced with tamer ones after Christianity was introduced here. Tamer, but maybe not as much fun."

Cat laughed, skimming the brochure. It said that the Guelaguetza festival, called Mondays on the Hill, was held every July to honor Centeotl, the goddess of corn. Tribes from the seven ancient regions of Oaxaca joined together to perform ceremonial dances and to celebrate.

As she and Aidan made their way into the already-packed amphitheater, lively guitar music filled the air. Men and women in traditional costumes stepped onto the circular stage and began dancing. While the men, in black hats and bright woven ponchos, led the women around the stage in an energetic dance, the women swirled their bright pink, purple, and yellow skirts. Cat thought the dancers looked like colored pinwheels from where she and Aidan sat in the stands. Once the song was over, nine-foot-tall figures took the stage, wearing oversize, papier-mâché heads with happy faces painted on them, and they started their own awkwardly funny dance.

"Those are called *mojigangos*," Aidan explained. "They're dancing puppets with people inside. They represent the Catholic saints that have taken the place of the ancient gods and goddesses of pre-Christian times."

"You really did your research for this, didn't you?" Cat said, impressed.

"I had help from a reliable but anonymous source." He smiled. "I'm trying to impress you with my vast wealth of knowledge. Is it working?"

"I think you mean Izzie's wealth of knowledge?" she guessed, then laughed at Aidan's sheepish nod. "But yes," she said, "it's working."

"Good," he said.

At the end of the performance a couple hours later, women dancers returned to the stage, balancing baskets of fruit and flowers on their heads. As the final song came to a close, the dancers threw pineapples from their baskets out to the audience.

"Heads up!" Aidan said, catching a flying fruit that came their way.

"My hero," Cat teased. She nodded toward the pineapple. "So, is that dinner?"

"It's one option," Aidan said as they moved through the crowd toward the exit. "Or I could take you to a place I had in mind. If you're willing to risk my choice of restaurant?"

Cat hesitated. She'd completely relaxed over the course of the afternoon, but would dinner be awkward? She

quickly pushed the thought away. She wasn't ready to call it a night yet. This was too much fun.

"Your choice of afternoon entertainment was great," she said, smiling. "So I'll take my chances on dinner, too."

She helped Aidan put the top down on the Jeep, and as they drove out of the city, she leaned back in her seat, taking in the beautiful scenery and the feel of the wind on her face. The road zigzagged in and out of the hillsides, until Aidan stopped at a charming little hacienda atop a hill overlooking the entire valley. Cat climbed out of the Jeep and a familiar, cozy scent wafted over her.

"I smell coffee," Cat said in surprise and delight.

"That's because we're on a coffee plantation," Aidan said, smiling. He showed her an outdoor patio set with colorful painted tables. Glowing red-and-yellow lanterns hung suspended from trees, and a mariachi band was playing music next to a trickling fountain.

"Now, you may be thinking that this looks a little too romantic for a not-date," Aidan said, reading Cat's thoughts exactly, "but it's not."

"That's a relief," Cat said, smiling. "Romance would be a major not-dating mistake."

"I totally agree." He grinned. "So we're going to work for our suppers."

Cat looked at him questioningly as they walked behind the hacienda, where they were greeted by other dinner goers, all picking coffee beans from trees.

"One basket of beans equals one dinner," Aidan explained.

Workers handed Aidan and Cat each a basket, and they started picking.

"You get points for originality." Cat laughed as she dropped beans into her basket. "But isn't this the kind of deforestation for coffee farms and development you were telling me destroys the rain forests?"

"Nope." Aidan shook his head. "This is shade-grown organic coffee. The beans are cultivated in the shade of the tropical forests, without disturbing the environment."

"Manual labor and fine dining." Cat grinned. "You know how to treat a girl."

They worked side by side for half an hour, talking while they worked, about Aidan's plans to swim in the Speedo Champion Series next year, and about Cat's love of Spanish. Cat even found herself telling him diving stories from when she lived in Scottsdale, but only after she'd made him promise not to bug her about joining the team in Boston. "Not one word. Scout's honor," he said with a grin. After they'd filled their baskets they sat down to dinner. They ate as the rosy sun sank behind the mountaintops, and then sampled the hacienda's coffee. Cat felt so comfortable with Aidan, she found herself laughing and talking happily, forgetting all of her earlier worries.

It was only during the drive home, under the moonlight and stars, that she felt a rush of panic again, this time

about their rapidly approaching not-date good night. Aidan hadn't tried to hold her hand or kiss her yet, but there would be the awkward moment when the question hung in the air. To kiss or not to kiss? She wasn't ready for that, even though, she had to admit, the thought had crossed her mind several times during the day.

But as they pulled up in front of the Canuls' door, Aidan proved that he was reading her mind, one more time.

He reached into the backseat. "I know it's not flowers, but here," he said, handing her the Guelaguetza pineapple, "this seems more appropriate for a not-date." He grinned. "And even though I know you're dying to make out with me, you should know that I never, ever kiss on a first not-date."

Cat laughed, all her nervousness vanishing as they got out of the car and Aidan handed her the Jeep key. "A handshake doesn't seem right either, though," she said. She gave him a hug, and when she pulled away, he was beaming.

"Will you be okay walking home?" she asked.

Aidan nodded. "It'll take only a few minutes, and it's a nice night." He grinned. "I think we're getting the hang of this not-dating thing. Should we try it again sometime?"

Cat smiled. "I'd really like that."

Chapter Nine

To: enginuity@email.com
From: lilmermaid @email.com

Hi Dad,

How's India? I loved the pictures you sent me. I can't believe you rode an elephant! Attached are some of my pics. No elephants, though, sorry! But there're a few rain forest monkeys instead. There's some of the orphan school, too. It's really taking shape. We're planting the but- terfly garden and setting up the playground now. I must

have planted about a hundred plumeria and Mexican sun-
flowers in the garden this week.

Once we get back from our trip to Puerto Ángel beach
this weekend, we'll start painting and decorating the classrooms. Sebastian just sent out invitations to the children at
the Oaxaca orphanage for the grand opening on August
19. (I can't believe it's only a couple weeks away!) Well, I
better finish packing for the beach. I've been waiting to see
the ocean since I stepped off the plane. It's about time.

Love,

Cat

Even though Cat had been serious about wanting to go on
another not-date with Aidan over the rest of the week,
between the paper on Palenque they had due and the
overtime they were putting in at the orphan school site, no
one had time to do anything except work and then fall
exhausted into bed each night. They'd lost a few days of
work because of heavy rains, so they were a little bit
behind schedule. But even with the crunch to make up
time, Sebastian still made sure this weekend was reserved
for another eco-education tour.

Cat had been looking forward to this trip all summer.
The group was headed five hours south of Oaxaca for a
weekend of snorkeling and marine biology studies at the
Centro Mexicano de la Tortuga, a research center for
Mexico's endangered sea turtles. At the end of the drive,

Cat knew there'd be miles and miles of open water and a whole ballet of dancing fish waiting for her.

The second she saw the coastline come into view from the bus window, her heart leaped. There were quiet lagoons where mangrove trees grew right out in the middle of the water, white sand beaches, and, best of all, ocean water and cresting white waves as far as she could see. She could almost feel the sand tickling her toes already.

"KitCat?" a voice said beside her. "Earth to Caitlin."

Cat blinked and looked up at Sabrina and Izzie, standing in the bus aisle. "Look at those waves," she said. "Have you ever seen ocean water that clear?"

"I see it, Miss Fish-out-of-Water," Sabrina said. "But don't grow gills yet. We have to tour the Turtle Center first, remember? We're here."

Cat had been so focused on the ocean, she hadn't even noticed the red-tile-roofed building sitting on the edge of the beach. She dragged her eyes away from the water and walked inside with the rest of the group, where they were greeted by one of the marine biologists working at the center. He gave them a tour of the research facilities, explaining the life cycles of turtles like the olive ridley, and showing them pools of adult turtles as well as the monitored nesting grounds where females laid their eggs. Cat took careful notes so she'd have lots of info for her paper on the Turtle Center.

"Unfortunately," the guide explained, "there aren't any hatchlings yet. But you can check our website daily. We announce the locations for nests along the coast where hatchlings have been sighted. Local villagers volunteer at the beaches to help get the little turtles into the water safely. Of course, the nesting sites are all heavily guarded against poachers these days as well."

"Does that mean no turtle soup?" Brian joked, but quickly stopped laughing when both Izzie and Aidan glared at him.

Cat was a little disappointed not to see any hatchlings, but Aidan was devastated.

"I can't believe it," he grumbled. "This is one of the only places left in the world where turtles hatch in their natural habitat. And we're missing it."

"Hey," Cat said. "We still have another hour here. Maybe something will happen."

But nothing did, and Sebastian finally announced it was time to move on to Puerto Ángel for snorkeling. While Aidan left the center reluctantly, Cat practically jumped on the bus and could barely sit still for the short ride to the beach.

She had her snorkel gear on before anyone else, and was in the water almost before Sebastian could lay out the ground rules. With instructions to watch out for sea snakes, jellyfish, and electric eels, she dove into the waves and swam out beyond the breakers to where schools of yellow-

and-blue parrot fish, angelfish, and even blowfish were swimming among the coral reefs. Time slipped away as she floated happily along, feeling completely at home amid the rolling surf.

She didn't know how many minutes had passed when she popped her head out of the water to take a break from her snorkel tube and saw Aidan swimming up beside her. She grinned, thinking he looked a little like an oversize bumblebee in his snorkel mask—a cute oversize bumble-bee. For the umpteenth time, she wished that last Saturday, when she'd had the chance, she had let him kiss her. When she'd recounted the whole day for Sabrina and Izzie later, she'd finally admitted that, as freaked as she was by the idea of liking Aidan, she was definitely feeling some chemistry.

"Are you over the hatchling no-show yet?" she asked Aidan.

"Swimming always puts me in a good mood." He smiled. "Besides, we might still see some tomorrow. In the mean-time, I think I have a better shot at seeing fish." He held up a banana. "Fish food. If we peel it, they will come."

The second Cat dipped the banana under the water, she and Aidan were surrounded. Hundreds of fish in a harmless feeding frenzy pulled at chunks of the banana as she held it out for them. Sabrina, Brian, Izzie, Pete, and Rachel swam out to join them, bringing more bananas with them. The water around them soon got so crammed,

it was hard to see anything but flashing fins. Sabrina squealed every time a parrot fish got close to her fingers, but Cat kept hoping she'd be able to touch one of them. Izzie called it quits after only a half hour, saying she was going to look for seashells instead, and then Pete started to look a little green around the gills.

"Seasickness," he moaned, before heading back into shore with Rachel and Izzie.

Snorkeling wasn't for everyone, but it was made for Cat. She gave the last remnants of her banana to the fish and then quietly split off from the others, swimming farther away from shore. Through her snorkeling mask, she saw a rainbow of colors below the waves, just like she'd always imagined. Taking a deep breath, she dove down toward the sandy ocean floor. She let the free-floating feeling engulf her until she couldn't hold her breath anymore, and then swam back up to the surface.

As she broke through the waves, she heard someone shouting in the distance. She looked toward the beach to see Sebastian waving his hands and motioning everyone in to shore.

"What's that all about?" she asked, rejoining the rest of the group.

"Jaws," Aidan said with theatrical menace.

"Yeah, right." Brian laughed. "Sebastian's probably just worried we forgot to put on sunblock or something."

"It's jellyfish!" Sebastian called out when they were

finally within hearing distance. "The coast guard spotted a large school of them just offshore. You'll have to beach it until they swim away."

Cat turned in the water to see that Sabrina and Brian were still a few hundred yards back, horsing around.

"You guys coming?" Cat called to them.

"We'll be there in a few!" Brian yelled back, and then dunked a giggling Sabrina playfully under the water.

Cat hesitated, wondering if she should play mom and swim back to get them. Sebastian had just yelled again for them to come in to shore, and Brian and Sabrina still had not moved. But it wasn't Cat's job to babysit the lovebirds, and she had a feeling if she pushed it, Brian wouldn't listen to her anyway. And since Sabrina always did everything Brian wanted to do, there'd be no hope convincing her otherwise.

So when Aidan said, "Up for a little friendly competition?" and took off toward the shore, Cat giggled and sped to follow. Sebastian could take care of Brian and Sabrina.

"I should've known better than to race a 4A swimmer," Cat gasped when she reached shore, trailing behind Aidan, trying to catch her breath.

"Looks like somebody needs to put in some serious pool time," Aidan teased. "You're a little out of practice."

"Hey, I may be out of practice swimming, but I'd kick your butt on the five-meter platform, and don't you forget it," Cat said.

"I'd like to see that someday," Aidan said.

They made their way to the blanket where Izzie and the rest of the gang were lounging, and started to dry off. Cat could see Sebastian motioning to Sabrina and Brian for the third time to swim in to shore, and it looked like they were finally moving, just taking their sweet old time at it. Cat shook her head, then flopped down next to Aidan just as a woman in a slender bikini sauntered by.

"I'm in heaven." Pete stared after her, a look of dreamy satisfaction on his face.

"I thought you were seasick," Cat said.

"Nah. I just wanted to get a good look at the land. I'm surrounded by beautiful, scantily clad women. It doesn't get much better than that." He grinned devilishly, right before Rachel smacked him.

"Sicko," she said.

Cat started to laugh, but it died in her throat when she heard sobbing and turned to see Sabrina being carried out of the waves in Brian's arms. Sebastian saw, too, and came running.

"What happened?" Cat cried, reaching Sabrina first.

"Jellyfish," Sabrina hissed through clenched teeth, holding her calf as tears ran down her face.

Brian laid her down on the sand while Sebastian examined the red welt swelling up on her leg. "What did it look like?" Sebastian asked.

Brian described the jellyfish sheepishly, running his

hands through his hair and looking by turns guilty and helpless.

"It sounds like a thimble jellyfish," Sebastian said. "They're not poisonous, but they have a nasty sting. Brian, why don't you get some ice from the snack kiosk for Sabrina? I have some cream in the first-aid kit on the bus that should help, too."

Cat had never seen Brian move so fast, but then, when he didn't reappear after ten minutes and Sabrina was still cringing from the sting, she went looking for him. And she found him all right, at the snack bar, chatting away without a care in the world to the same beautiful, bikini-clad girl Cat had seen walking down the beach earlier. Unbelievable. Brian was actually flirting with another girl while Sabrina was on the beach crying over a sting that was partly his fault to begin with. Cat had heard him make skeevy jokes about other girls before, but this was too much.

"The ice, Brian?" Cat said, not even trying to hide the irritation in her voice.

"Oh yeah!" he said, laughing. "Here you go." He handed the pack of ice to Cat. "I'll be right over."

She stomped away, fuming. What a loser he was turning out to be. She'd been willing to give him a chance, for Sabrina's sake, but the side of him she'd just seen scratched any hope of that ever happening again. And poor Sabrina. This could be a huge red flag for her. If

Brian's flirting ever turned into something more, Sabrina would be left heartbroken.

"Where's Brian?" Sabrina asked when Cat returned with the ice.

"Bathroom," Cat said quickly. She hated herself for lying. She'd have to talk to Sabrina about this, but not now. She didn't want to cause her any more tears today.

The ice pack and cream Sebastian had given Sabrina seemed to work, because soon Sabrina was back to smiling and making weak jokes with Cat.

"I'll go get you a sandwich and some soda," Cat offered when Sabrina had cheered up a bit. Cat had ulterior motives, too, because Brian was finally walking toward them, and she couldn't deal with playing nice with him right now.

"Thanks," Sabrina said to her, but she must have seen a hint of anger on Cat's face, because she nodded toward Brian and whispered to Cat, "It wasn't his fault, you know. I wanted to stay in the water, too."

Cat looked at Sabrina's pleading eyes and sighed. "I know."

But that night, after she and Sabrina had settled into their *palapa*, the small thatched hut that was one of ten Sebastian had reserved on the beach for the program, everything that had happened earlier kept running through her mind. She was so glad that Izzie had graciously offered to bunk with Rachel this weekend so that she could room with Sabrina, especially now that Sabrina wasn't feeling too hot. She grabbed her journal and let out a stream of venting:

August 5, 10:30 P.M.

Poor Sabrina. I'm worried about her. She's lying on her cot with an ice pack on her leg, and she only just now fell asleep. She kept downplaying the whole thing today, but her calf is still the color of a tomato! I'm trying not to blame Brian for this, but every time I look over at Sabrina I get even madder at him.

Note to Future Daughters (not that I'm having future daughters, because I'm never getting married): Never trust a guy who takes you swimming with venomous sea creatures. He may tell you it's perfectly safe, but you'll get stung.

It was when the sky was turning gray with a faint light the next morning that Cat heard the quiet knocking. Sabrina was still sound asleep, so Cat tiptoed over to the door. Cracking it open, she saw Aidan, fully dressed, with his nature sketchbook tucked under his arm.

"What are you doing up?" Cat whispered.

"Come for a walk with me?" Aidan asked, his eyes bright with excitement.

Cat checked the clock in the room. "It's five o'clock in the morning," she said.

"I know, I know," Aidan said hurriedly. "You really don't want to miss this."

"Okay," Cat said. "One minute."

She threw on shorts and a T-shirt, splashed some cold water on her face, and brushed her teeth. She didn't bother with a mirror check. She probably had bed head, but at this hour of the morning, she couldn't care less, and she knew Aidan wouldn't mind. He wasn't the kind of guy who cared about stuff like that. It was one of the things she liked about him so much.

Once they were outside, Aidan took off walking so fast, it was tough for her to keep up. When he turned to her, holding out his hand, she took it without even the slightest hesitation, and they both grinned as she did.

"Can I know where we're going?" she asked. "Or is this a kidnapping?"

"Just trust me." Aidan said.

Cat laughed. "Famous last words."

He led her away from the *palapas* and onto the cool sand of the beach below. The morning sky was getting brighter, and soon the sun would peek over the horizon.

"There." Aidan pointed to a spot in the sand that seemed, strangely, to be moving.

"I don't see—" Cat started, but then she did. Hundreds of tiny turtles, crawling out of the sand and scrambling with their miniature flippers toward the breaking waves.

She laughed with delight. "But how did you know they'd be here?"

"I've been logged on to the Centro Mexicano de la Tortuga's website since last night," Aidan said. "I kept checking. The announcement was posted a half hour ago."

They carefully stepped closer to the turtles. Some park rangers were already on the scene, picking up the turtles and wading knee-deep with them into the ocean water.

"You can help if you'd like," one of them said to Cat and Aidan. "By carrying them to the water, we're trying to protect them from predators. But once they're in the water, they're on their own."

That was all Cat and Aidan needed to hear to set to work. Cat picked up the first turtle, no bigger than the palm of her hand. Its waving flippers tickled her hand as she walked down to the water with it. She slipped off her sandals and stepped into the warm waves, and when she was knee-deep, she cupped both her hands and dipped the baby turtle into the water. She laughed as it immediately launched itself off her palms and scooted in little jerking strides out into the deep. Seagulls were circling

overhead, and, sadly, some of the turtles got eaten while they were swimming away. But not as many as would have been if the turtles had remained on the sand.

The sky streaked with orange light as Cat went back and forth across the beach, picking up turtle after turtle. As every one swam away from her, she made a silent wish that it would stay safe. Finally, as a bright red sun crested over the ocean, Cat stood next to Aidan, watching the last of the turtles swim away.

"How many do you think will make it?" she asked.

"It's tough out there," Aidan said. "Only about one in ten thousand hatchlings makes it in the wild, but the strong ones will survive." He took her hand and gave it a squeeze. "We should head back."

He turned to walk up the beach, but Cat stopped him. "Wait. Aidan?" She kept hold of his hand and pulled him back to her, smiling. She blushed as she said the next words, the words she'd wanted to say for a week. "So...what's the rule for not-kissing?"

"On a not-date?" He grinned, taking her face gently in his hands. "Not-kisses are definitely allowed."

Cat had never been not-kissed before, but in her opinion, it was way better than the real thing.

Of course, when Cat walked into the *palapa* after she and Aidan left the beach, it took about a millisecond for Sabrina to guess what had happened.

"You kissed him, didn't you?" she shrieked when she saw Cat's glowing face. "I knew you'd cave!"

"Correction. I not-kissed him. But it's no big deal," Cat tried to tell her.

"Come on! You never kiss anyone!" Sabrina cried. "This is a huge deal!" She paced the room, smiling. "Just think of all the double-dating possibilities! We'll have so much fun. We can go out to eat together. And when we get to Mexico City next weekend, we'll have such a blast. We *have* to go out dancing."

"What about your leg?" Cat asked, pointing to Sabrina's bandage.

"Please." Sabrina rolled her eyes. "It barely stings anymore. It'll be way better by then. There's no way Brian and I are sitting out the club scene, and you and Aidan aren't either."

Cat laughed, but then suddenly got serious. "Sabrina, about what happened yesterday..." She paused, knowing she was about to tread on thin ice. "What I mean is...are you happy with Brian?"

"What?" Sabrina laughed nervously, turning away to pack her bag for the trip home. "Of course I am. I love him."

Cat nodded. "I know. But I'm a little worried. Sometimes he doesn't seem so...so into you."

Sabrina frowned. "Just because he made a mistake yesterday doesn't mean he's not into me. He must have said he was sorry about fifty times last night." She sighed.

"Could you just try to get to know him better? I know you'll see how great he is."

Cat sighed. "I'm glad he apologized. It's just that, sometimes I think that he doesn't treat you as well as he should."

Sabrina glared at Cat, then began throwing the rest of the clothes into her bag. "I knew you didn't like him, right from the beginning. You get this look on your face whenever he talks to you." Her voice was rising. "I just wanted you two to be friends."

"I know," Cat said. "But—"

"This is just so typical. I find a guy who I can have more than a fling with, and you try to ruin it by finding something wrong with him. You know, just because you're afraid to date doesn't mean you get free rein to criticize people who can actually do it."

"What are you talking about?" Cat cried. "I'm not afraid. Aidan and I are—"

"Not-dating," Sabrina said. "Give me a break. That's a total cop-out, and you know it. You might have kissed Aidan, but you two still haven't had a real date. You're so afraid of dating that you can't even call it what it is."

"Oh, so *you're* living in reality and I'm not?" Cat cried. "At least I haven't had a whole string of pointless boy toys. You can't even see Brian for what he really is!"

"And what's that?" Sabrina shot back, grabbing her bag

and heading for the door. "Go on and say it! You know you want to."

"He's an a—" The word died in her throat, and she stared at the floor, not able to say what she knew would make the rift between her and Sabrina even worse.

"I knew you wouldn't have the guts," Sabrina said. "Thanks for the confirmation." She walked out, slamming the door behind her.

Cat stared after her with a mix of anger and heavy, sinking dread. Now what? She didn't want to go through the rest of the semester fighting with her, but she couldn't just let Sabrina walk into a huge mistake with Brian. Then again, maybe she was wrong about him. She hadn't seen him do anything besides talk to that girl. But if she wasn't wrong? Once they got back to Oaxaca, she'd have to bring it up again—it was just too important to let slide.

Chapter Ten

It turned out that once they got back to Oaxaca, there was never a good time to talk to Sabrina about Brian. Cat had gone out on a couple more not-dates with Aidan in the past week, but the more time she'd spent with him, the less she'd seen Sabrina. She'd tried inviting Sabrina and Brian to join her and Aidan for dinner one night, but Sabrina had said no, explaining that she and Brian had to finish their Puerto Ángel papers before the Mexico City eco-tour. When Cat saw her at the work site, Sabrina was quieter than usual, too, especially around her. She was always smiling, but Cat could see a tightness in her smile that had not been there before.

The last dig came as Cat boarded the bus for Mexico City on Friday morning. Sabrina had given her a weak smile, but hadn't given any indication that she wanted Cat and Aidan to sit in the empty seats across from her and Brian. Instead, Cat chose a pair of seats near Izzie, Pete, and Rachel. Izzie and Aidan quickly got into a deep conversation about endangered species, and Pete started his normal Don Juan routine as Rachel scolded him. Cat tried to smile and join in the fun. It was still going to be a great trip, but she couldn't help feeling a little sad that her best friend was not sitting near her to share in it. Her spirits lifted, though, when she caught her first glimpse of Mexico City.

The booming city was not nearly as small, or as charming, as Oaxaca, but it looked exciting. It went on for miles, and the gold-gilded domed cathedrals and Baroque-style buildings were a breathtaking sight, especially as the setting sun glinted off of them.

"Imagine how this capital must have looked when Hernán Cortés marched into it with his army," Sebastian said as the bus drove them into the historic downtown area. "Centuries ago, the original Aztec city center rested on an island in the middle of Lake Texcoco. It was an amazing empire, impressive enough to warrant the name

City of the Gods. But that was before the Spanish destroyed the buildings and filled in the lake."

The bus slowed, coming to a stop in front of a beautiful Baroque building with "Casa Bonita" in gold lettering across an awning out front. "This hotel is a special treat," Sebastian said. "It's one of the oldest in the city. Once we check in, we'll have dinner in the hotel restaurant. Afterward, you're free to explore the city. I ask only that you report in to me by midnight tonight. Be safe, but have fun."

As Cat stepped off the bus, she wondered just how much fun she'd have with the awkwardness between her and Sabrina still hanging over her head. Her new goal would be to find a good distraction from it, and quick.

Two hours and several platefuls of tamales later, it was Izzie who came up with the distraction.

"So, what's the most fun thing to do in Mexico City at night?" Cat made the mistake of asking her when they'd settled into their room after dinner. She was back to sharing a room with Izzie this trip, since she'd been hesitant about asking Sabrina to room with her, afraid of the answer she might get. Sabrina hadn't said a word about it either, so Cat assumed this was how she wanted things to be.

"*Es fácil.* That's easy." Izzie broke into a huge grin, her normally serious eyes lit up playfully. "Salsa dancing."

Cat groaned. "I was hoping for something that didn't

involve humiliation? The last time I tried dancing was with Greg Jones at a school dance in sixth grade. I broke his toe."

"You stepped on it?" Izzie asked.

"Stomped on it…on purpose," Cat said, and at Izzie's shocked expression added in self-defense, "Hey! He tried to kiss me!"

Izzie laughed. "I don't see you complaining about kissing *Aidan*."

Cat blushed. "What can I say? Kissing's grown on me since poor, unfortunate Greggie. But that's beside the point. I don't know if Aidan's a dancer. And I *know* I'm not."

"I'll teach you," Izzie said simply. "You can't spend a summer in Mexico without learning to salsa. Just don't break any more toes."

Cat giggled, but then felt a pang of sadness remembering that, just a week ago, Sabrina had been thrilled with the idea of going out dancing together once they got here. But Sabrina had sat with Brian during dinner and headed straight back to her own room afterward. There didn't seem to be much hope of convincing her to join them, but Cat didn't want to give up yet. Besides, this was the first time Cat had ever seen Izzie willing to cut loose. Catching a glimpse of the party-girl side of Izzie, if there really was one, would be worth a trip to a dance club.

"All right," Cat said. "I'll go. But I can't make any promises about any broken toes."

"As long as Aidan's the only one trying to kiss you, that won't be a problem," Izzie said with a smile.

"I can't argue with that." Cat smiled. She opened her duffel and stared at the red-and-blue woven wrap skirt, which she'd bought yesterday afternoon, lying right on top. It was a total impulse buy. She'd seen it when she was walking by the Mercado de Abastos in Oaxaca, and before she knew it, for the first time in her life, she'd purchased a skirt of her own free will. It was the color that sold her on it. That ocean blue was her favorite. Besides, Aidan had never seen her in a skirt, and she liked the idea of surprising him.

Now she went into the bathroom and pulled it on. The skirt came up above her knees, highlighting her toned diver's legs and waist. It wasn't too flowery or frilly, and the cut made it look a little sporty, with just a hint of femininity, which she liked. And with a fitted sleeveless top to match, she actually looked... pretty?

"So?" she asked Izzie, coming out of the bathroom. "Is this a good salsa outfit?"

Izzie grinned and nodded. *"Perfecto."*

Cat slipped on the earrings Sabrina had given her. "Now," she said, "the trick will be convincing Aidan to come along."

Izzie smiled. "He won't need any convincing."

"Are you kidding?" Aidan said when Cat asked. "I'd be an

idiot not to go." He grinned. "If I stayed here, I'd be dying of jealousy thinking of all the guys dancing with you."

"There isn't much chance of that happening." Cat laughed. "Not the way I dance."

"If the way you dance is anything like the way you dive," Aidan said, "there's nothing to worry about."

"It's not," Cat said, "so feel free to worry. My face could meet the dance floor at any point in the evening."

"Not if I'm there to catch you," he said gallantly, then laughed. "Besides, I'll never notice a few missed steps on the dance floor when you look so...so..."

"Girly?" Cat asked, laughing.

"Amazing," Aidan finished.

"Thanks." Cat blushed. She wasn't used to getting compliments like this. But she liked the way the skirt moved with her as she walked, and even if she went back to her cargo pants tomorrow morning, for tonight, she felt feminine in a good way. "I figured a date with you was worthy of breaking my no-skirts rule for one night."

"Wait a minute." Aidan smiled. "Did you just say what I thought you said? A date?"

Cat felt her blush turning one shade redder. She hadn't meant to say "date." It had slipped out when she wasn't thinking. But now it was out there, and, amazingly, she showed no signs of panic. Maybe she was ready for this...finally. No more copping out. She smiled at Aidan. "If it's a real date, do I get a real kiss?"

Aidan slipped his arms around her waist and kissed her softly. "You didn't even have to ask," he whispered.

"Izzie's meeting us down in the lobby in ten minutes," Cat said as she pulled away. "But there's something I need to do before we go. I'll be right back."

Cat took a deep breath as she knocked on Sabrina's door, then waited. Nothing. If Sabrina blew her off tonight, she wasn't sure how they would finish off their semester. But they had a history together, and she refused to let it all fall apart.

She knocked one more time and heard a shuffling, then silence.

"Sabrina?" she called through the door. "I know you're there. I can see your feet through the crack under the door. Open up. Please."

There was an audible sigh, and the door opened on Sabrina, staring half annoyed, half angry at Cat.

"Hey," Cat started, giving a tentative smile.

"Hey," Sabrina muttered. Her eyes fell on Cat's skirt for a few seconds, and then shifted to the floor.

"I came to see if you wanted to go out with us tonight," Cat said. "Izzie and I are getting a group together. Pete and Rachel are coming, too. And we'd—no, I'd—love it if you and Brian came along."

Sabrina stared at the floor, biting her lip. "I don't think

that's such a good idea," she said. She started to shut the door, but Cat stopped her.

"I know you're still mad at me, but can we please forget the whole thing? I'm sorry I said anything." She sighed. "Can we just go back to the way everything was before?"

"Things can't be exactly like they were in Arizona, Cat," Sabrina said matter-of-factly. "I'm not breaking up with Brian."

Cat nodded. "I know, and I want to get to know him better. You're probably right. I wasn't giving him a fair chance."

"You weren't," Sabrina said. She paused, digging her toes into the carpet. "You're wearing a skirt."

Cat smiled. "Yup, *and* it's free of synthetics and chemical dyes. Aren't you proud?"

A small smile crossed Sabrina's lips. "Well, I *have* been telling you to buy organic for years."

"Just don't breathe a word of this to my mom," Cat said. "She'd start dragging me into Ann Taylor stores all over Boston." She tilted her head. "And...I'm wearing the earrings you gave me." She did a little turn in the hallway. "What do you think?"

Sabrina rolled her eyes, but then broke into a grin. "I think it's about time you got in touch with your glam-girl side."

"I'll do more than that," Cat said. At every junior high

and high school dance since the Greg Jones disaster, Cat had sat on the sidelines. No matter how much Sabrina begged and pleaded, she would never get out on the floor. "If you come with us tonight, I'll even give this whole salsa thing a try." Cat waited, letting this new revelation sink in with Sabrina.

"Now that"—Sabrina laughed—"is something I've got to see. I'll be ready in ten."

Bar León, Izzie explained as they walked into the club, was one of the best-known salsa clubs in Mexico City. And the minute Cat saw the dancers out on the floor, she understood why. These dancers were no amateurs. They made every step with certainty and grace as the lively chords of the salsa music washed over them. It looked beautiful, but also totally terrifying.

"We're going to try to dance with *them*?" Cat asked doubtfully.

"Not *try to* dance," Sabrina said, giggling as Brian nuzzled her neck. "*Going to* dance with them."

"I think I could've settled for some flan and a swim in the hotel pool," Cat said.

"But where's the fun in that?" Izzie grinned. "*Camarón que se duerme, se lo lleva la corriente.* The shrimp that falls asleep gets washed away by the current."

"More like, the girl who trips on the dance floor gets trampled by salsa zealots," Cat retorted.

"Pesimista," Izzie said. *"Ven conmigo.* Come on. We'll just watch first."

She led them to a table at the edge of the dance floor. Sabrina and Brian stayed seated only long enough for a quick drink, and then they hit the dance floor, but Cat needed to mentally prepare herself before giving it a try.

"Has Sabrina ever salsaed before?" Aidan asked Cat as they watched them.

"Not that I know of," Cat said. "But she learns fast." Sabrina looked great at just about anything she did, and this was no different. Even though Brian fumbled at first, just dancing with Sabrina was enough to make him look good out there.

Izzie suddenly stood up. *"Vamanos,* Casanova," she said, grabbing Pete by the hand. "I'm going to teach you how to dance."

"I knew you liked me," Pete said, grinning so widely that his cheeks lifted his glasses slightly off his nose.

Salsa music filled the air, and Cat's toes were tapping by the time she saw Izzie and Pete taking their second turn around the dance floor. Izzie was a terrific dancer, and, even though she'd started off leading, Pete, amazingly, seemed to be holding his own. Rachel had been asked to dance by a cute blond, too, and they didn't look half bad out there, either.

"Izzie's good," Aidan said beside her. "But I think I can do better."

Cat gave a half snort of laughter. "Oh, really? Since when do you know how to salsa?"

"Are you doubting me?" Aidan asked, faking shock. "That sounded like a challenge." He stood up and took her hand. "Let's go."

Cat giggled as he led her to the dance floor. Okay, so they'd give it a try, trip all over each other, and end up back in the booth. But as soon as her feet hit the floor, Aidan grabbed her tightly by the waist and spun her in one graceful movement. Then, before she even had time to blink, he snapped her back to his side and, with one hand firmly on the small of her back, began moving smoothly, flawlessly to the music.

"There are three basic steps of salsa," he said, trying to be serious, but cracking a proud smile. "When I move my right foot back, you move your left foot forward. Then put your feet together. After that, we move the other set of feet in the opposite directions."

She struggled with the steps, moving the wrong foot at the wrong time, and stomping on Aidan's feet in the process. "You know how some people have two left feet?" she said, laughing. "I have three or four."

"Good thing I'm wearing Cat-proof shoes." Aidan laughed. "Just relax and let me lead."

Once Cat had the hang of them, the basic steps slowly got easier, and then the fun really started. Aidan spun her around the dance floor without tripping up one time. She didn't even need to think about her feet; he did all the work. She flew by Izzie and Pete, and saw Izzie staring in disbelief as they passed.

"Who taught you how to dance like this?" Cat asked, when she'd had a chance to catch her breath.

Aidan spun her again. "My stepmother," he said.

"You never told me you had a stepmother," Cat said, surprised.

"It's no big deal." Aidan shrugged. "My dad and mom got divorced when I was ten. And thank God they did, or they might've killed each other before I hit puberty. My dad married my stepmom six years ago. I don't really think of her as a stepparent anymore, so I don't usually point it out to people. When she was younger, she was a professional Broadway dancer."

"Who was obviously terrific at salsa," Cat added.

Aidan grinned. "She always says that every guy should know how to open doors for ladies and lead them on a dance floor. So how am I doing?"

"Great on both accounts." Cat kissed him. "She must be a fab teacher." She hesitated before asking her next question. "And what about your real mom?"

"She lives in New Jersey," Aidan said, "and I spend one weekend a month with her."

"I bet it's nice to have all three of them so close by," Cat

said, thinking about her dad, thousands of miles away most months of the year.

"It is," Aidan said. "I think I'm pretty lucky. A lot of people have only two parents, and sometimes parents are messed up, you know, whether they're step or real. But I have three great ones."

Cat nodded, letting that slowly sink in. She'd never really thought about family from that perspective before. Her family was so different from Aidan's. His stepmother sounded really cool. She wasn't some straight-and-narrow university prof who ate doughnuts with utensils, that was for sure. But then again, that same university prof had gone out of his way to make sure she got her favorite dessert on her birthday, too. She brushed away the confusing thoughts and tried to focus on dancing again. And as soon as she did, she stepped on Aidan's toe.

The music set ended, and Aidan went to get some drinks while Cat waded through the thick crowd to find the restroom. She found it in a slightly quieter corner of the club, and hurried down the narrow, dimly lit hallway. She didn't even see the snuggling couple tucked away behind one of the phone booths until she stumbled into them.

"I'm so sorry," she muttered, trying to move past them as quickly as possible. But they hadn't even broken their lip-lock. And even in the half-light, she immediately recognized Brian's red hair and tall frame as he cuddled the petite blonde at his side. Wait a minute. Petite *blonde*?

Sabrina's auburn waves could never be mistaken for the bleached blonde Cat saw wrapping her arms around Brian's waist. She froze, doing a double take. Yup, that was definitely Brian, but that was definitely *not* Sabrina. What did he think he was doing, making out with another girl? And where was Sabrina?

She stormed back to the table to find Aidan waiting with the drinks.

"Hey, is everything okay?" he asked when he saw Cat's frown. "You're tugging on your hair."

"You're not going to believe this," Cat said. "I just saw Brian cheating on Sabrina."

Aidan sighed and shook his head. "That sucks for Sabrina, but I believe it. That day when we went snorkeling in Puerto Ángel, he had his eyes on a lot more than the fish. He was ogling girls on the beach the whole afternoon."

"Too bad he can't get points on his Ivy League application for including 'chronic flirt' under his list of achievements." Cat stood up. "I have to find Sabrina."

"What are you going to tell her?" he asked.

"The truth," she said. "She deserves to hear it, and she'll never get it out of him."

"Do you want me to come with you?" Aidan asked.

No," she said. "That's okay." She gave him a reassuring smile. "Have fun. Dance with Rachel and Izzie. You'll knock them off their feet."

"You know it." He laughed. "I'll be here if you need me."

"Thanks," she said, feeling very lucky that she'd found a guy who seemed like the type who would be there, no matter how many bleached blondes crossed his path.

She found Sabrina sitting in a half-circle-shaped booth by herself, wearing a strained smile and trying to look like she was having a good time. Cat could see she was failing miserably.

"I've been looking all over for you," Cat said. "Can we talk?"

"Sure!" Sabrina said, a little too brightly. Then she looked past Cat and into the crowd of dancers. "Have you seen Brian? He went to get drinks a while ago." She giggled. "Do you think Izzie dragged him out onto the dance floor? That girl can seriously salsa!"

Cat sat down at the booth, sighing. "Sabrina, I did see him a few minutes ago," she said. "But not with Izzie. He was with another girl I haven't seen before." She took a deep breath. "And they were making out."

Sabrina stared at the table, biting her trembling lip.

"I'm so sorry," Cat whispered, slipping an arm around her shoulders.

Sabrina jerked away and glared at her, furious. "That's such a crappy thing to say, and you know it's not true."

Cat's mouth dropped open. "But I just saw the whole thing. He was kissing her!"

"Brian would never do anything to hurt me," Sabrina said, tears in her eyes. "You're just jealous because I've been spending so much time with him. That's why you always cop an attitude around him. But to make up such an awful story just to get me to break up with him? I thought you were a better person than that."

"I'm trying to look out for you!" Cat cried. "He's a total asshole, I know. I saw him flirting with a girl at the beach that day you got stung by the jellyfish, too. I just didn't know how to tell you before, and—"

"You're lying," Sabrina said, seething.

Cat stared at her, not believing what she was hearing. She knew Sabrina was hurt, but to blame her for every-thing *and* call her a liar?

"Look, if you want to keep on believing that Brian's a terrific guy, go right ahead," Cat said, fuming. "But don't insult me. I've never lied to you about anything, and I cer-tainly wouldn't start over a guy."

"I don't have to listen to this." Sabrina slid over and stood up. "I can't believe I wasted so much time being friends with someone like you!"

And before Cat could say another word, Sabrina disap-peared into the crowd. When Aidan found her ten minutes later, Cat was still at the booth, wondering how her whole conversation with Sabrina had gone so horribly wrong.

Two days and a half-dozen Mexico City tourist sites still

couldn't take Cat's mind off her Friday-night fight with Sabrina. Even on Sunday morning, as she explored the Museo de Arte Moderno with Izzie and Aidan before the drive back to Oaxaca, her blowup with Sabrina kept haunting her.

"I just don't understand how she could think it was all my fault," Cat told Izzie and Aidan as they stood in front of Frida Kahlo's painting *The Two Fridas*. This room in the museum was entirely dedicated to the works of Frida Kahlo and Diego Rivera, two of Mexico's greatest artists.

"She doesn't really believe it was your fault," Izzie said. "She's just not ready to believe it was Brian's fault yet, either."

"She's never been this mad at me before," Cat said, doodling absentmindedly in her study guide in the space where her notes on the museum should've been. "Maybe I shouldn't have told her."

"It's not much of a friendship if you can't be honest with each other," Aidan said. "Besides, if she'd found out from someone else, it would've been way worse."

"Worse how?" Cat asked. "She couldn't even look at me yesterday."

Yesterday, the group had gone to Teotihuacán, the site of one of the greatest ancient Aztec cities in Mexico. Cat walked through the ruins with Aidan and Izzie, trying to focus on the lecture, but it weighed on her to see Sabrina and Brian staying at an obvious safe distance from her.

Sabrina had circles under her eyes, the telltale sign that she'd been crying. Every time Cat tried to make eye contact with her, Sabrina turned away. Brian seemed like his usual self, grinning and cracking jokes with his J.Crew crowd, and being extra-cuddly with Sabrina. Cat had no doubt he'd come up with a very logical story to explain away all of the accusations she'd brought up with Sabrina the night before. Whatever he'd told Sabrina, she apparently believed every word. Cat had turned into a disloyal, bitchy friend in Sabrina's eyes, and she had no idea what she could say or do to fix that now.

"Give her a few more days," Aidan said, giving Cat's hand a squeeze. "She'll come around."

"I don't know," Cat whispered. She studied the painting in front of her, halfheartedly scribbling down a few notes about it. Two identical faces of Frida Kahlo peered out of the canvas, but each Frida wore a completely different outfit.

"She's wearing the native dress of her people here," Izzie said, pointing to the Frida in a colorful blue-and-green skirt and blouse. "And European clothing here." She motioned to Frida's other self, dressed in a traditional high-necked white dress. "She's showing how she is torn by two identities, two selves."

Cat stared at the picture. Ever since she'd moved to Boston, she'd felt like she'd left half of herself behind in Arizona. Her Boston half was lost and lonely, but the Arizona half still had her old diving friends and a place on

the team, and still had a best friend in Sabrina. Sabrina had been the tie linking the two halves together.

"You know what's ridiculous?" Cat said. "Sabrina and I got along so great in Arizona. I just wanted us to have one more summer like that, and look what happened."

Aidan squeezed her hand. "Nothing ever stays the same, Cat. You've just got to take it as it comes."

Cat laughed. "You sound like my mother."

Aidan groaned. "And that's my cue to shut up."

"No," Cat said. "I'm starting to think she sort of knew what she was talking about. But if you ever meet her, don't tell her I said so."

Aidan laughed. "Your secret's safe with me."

Cat tried to enjoy the rest of the day, but a sense of panic was settling over her. There was only one more week until the end of the semester—one more week for her and Sabrina to mend their friendship. Because once she got back to Boston, it might be too late.

Chapter Eleven

Her friendship with Sabrina might have been falling apart, but at least it was comforting to see the orphan school coming together. It had been a few days since their trip to Mexico City, and Cat had been working frantically, along with the rest of the students, to put the finishing touches on the school. The group was leaving for their final eco-education tour to Acapulco this afternoon, and Cat, Aidan, and Izzie were putting the last coat of paint on the science classroom walls beforehand.

They'd picked a bright sunshiny yellow for the back-ground, and on top of that, they'd been working to create

a bright collage. Aidan had transferred some of his animal drawings from his sketchbook onto the wall, and Cat and Izzie were helping to fill them in with paint. There were howler monkeys, mangrove trees, a jaguar. Cat's contribution was a nest of hatching sea turtles. She'd never been good at drawing, but Aidan had shown her how to draw a basic turtle using simple geometric shapes, and in the end, they didn't look half bad. The whole room was taking on the vibrant colors of the tropical forests, mountains, and seasides of Mexico. But it was a scramble to finish. The Helping Hands bus was picking them up in the *zócalo* at four P.M. sharp for the six-hour drive to Acapulco, and the painting had to be done before then.

This trip to Acapulco was really less like an eco-tour and more like a mini-postfinals vacation, since grades were going to be determined by the comprehensive final, which everyone had just taken yesterday afternoon. Cat had stayed up far into the A.M. hours more than once since their Mexico City trip to prep for the final, reviewing all of her lecture notes on the archaeological sites they'd seen, the natural-science lessons they'd had at the beach and in the rain forests and coffee plantations, and Mexican history and culture. Going into the test, she'd thought she had a pretty good grasp of the material. But now, as she dipped her brush into her pot of green paint, she had a moment of doubt.

"I don't think I spelled Frida Kahlo's name right on the

essay yesterday," she said as she finished one baby turtle and moved on to another.

"You did," Aidan said.

"I can't remember what date I put down for the start of the Mexican Revolution, either," she said miserably.

"Cat," Aidan said. "Would you stop worrying? I'm sure you aced it."

"But what if I didn't?" she said.

"I thought you didn't care about your grades?" Izzie said as she finished filling in a mangrove tree.

"I don't," Cat said immediately, forgetting for a second that these weren't her parents she was talking to. "I mean, I do care…a little."

"You care a lot," Aidan corrected. "Which is why you're going to get an A."

Cat couldn't deny it. The fact was that she cared…big-time. She cared about what she'd seen in Mexico, and she was going to do right by it, even if that meant ditching her plan to flunk out of school. Besides, she had to face it…getting good grades came more naturally to her than getting bad ones. And if flunking out wasn't going to get her sent back to Arizona, which she knew now it wasn't, then she might as well give herself some satisfaction by trying her best in school again.

"Done," she said, standing back to admire her turtles.

"*Yo también,*" Izzie said. "Let's clean up so we can get packed in time for the bus to Acapulco."

"See you tonight," Cat said, waving to Aidan, who was still focused on adding some more spots to the jaguar on the wall.

As she and Izzie walked through the school, Cat realized that the next time they saw it would be next Saturday for the grand opening.

"I can't believe it's finished," Cat said, admiring the hallway bulletin boards decorated with numbers, letters, colors, and calendars. "All of our hard work paid off."

"Sebastian told me that the orphanage is busing one hundred children out for the opening," Izzie said.

"I can't wait to see the looks on their faces." They stepped out into the bright sunshine and passed the finished playground, with its red, blue, and yellow swings; the shiny new slide; and the jungle gym. "Do you think they'll like it?"

Izzie grinned. "They'll love it. Of all the projects I've worked on in the last three years, this one is my favorite."

As they reached the Jeep, Cat saw Sabrina and Brian working in the butterfly garden, pulling weeds and watering the flowers. Brian was using the water more for himself than the flowers, spraying the hose over his head and shoulders to cool off.

Sabrina looked up and caught Cat's eye for a split second, but then dropped her head quickly.

"Sabrina's still not speaking to you?" Izzie asked Cat.

Cat shook her head, sighing. "But I'm holding out for a miracle."

"Maybe we should stop at the basilica to ask for *la virgen*'s help," Izzie offered, half seriously.

"It's not a bad idea," Cat said. "I'll take all the help I can get."

"En Mexico," Izzie said, *"nosotros decimos que no hay mal que por bien no venga."*

"There is no bad from which good doesn't come," Cat translated. "I wish it were easier for me to believe that."

"¿Y por qué no?" Izzie asked. "If your mom hadn't remarried, you would never have moved to Boston. And if you hadn't moved to Boston, your parents would never have let you come on this trip. And if you had never come on this trip, you would never have met Aidan. Or Rachel and Pete. Or me. And...you would never have known how good *chapulines* taste."

Cat laughed. "True enough. But I might have been able to live without the fried grasshoppers."

Abril heated an afternoon snack of leftover tamales for Cat and Izzie while they packed for the trip, and Cat logged on to her laptop to write a quick note to her own mom before slipping it into her bag to take with her. In her in box, though, she found a message from an address she didn't recognize. It was only when she opened it that she realized

it was from Ted. That was strange. She'd never gotten an e-mail from him before. It was always her mom who sent the e-mails from home. She was even more surprised when she read through it.

To: lilmermaid@email.com

From: historybuff@email.com

Subject: Your bedroom

Hi Cat,

I'm sure you weren't expecting to get an e-mail from me, but even a boring history professor can sneak in a surprise now and then. And yes, I know you think I'm boring, and that you think it's weird that I eat my doughnuts with a knife and fork (the look on your face that day did not escape my attention). But I'm still hopeful you'll change your mind about me someday (about the boring part, that is; I know cutting doughnuts is weird, but after I reached a certain age, I stopped trying to fight my eccentricities).

Your mom and I are looking forward to seeing you on Sunday, but in the meantime, I thought you'd like to see a picture of your bedroom (attached). I took the liberty of repainting it. (Don't worry. Your mom moved all of your things beforehand. I didn't touch anything except the walls. I promise.) That old pasty beige color was boring. That's one thing we might both agree on. I hope you like the new

color. It's just a little something to say welcome home . . . in
advance. And I mean it from the bottom of my heart, Cat.

Ted

Cat glared at the screen, fuming. How dare her mom and
Ted go into her bedroom and mess with her stuff. How
dare her mom let Ted paint her walls. He had probably
painted them some god-awful puke green or something,
like that murky duck-pond color that profs always had on
their office walls.

She double-clicked on the attachment, dreading what
was about to pop up. Then she grabbed her cell phone
from her bag, ready to dial her mom's number and launch
into a fit as soon as she picked up the phone. But when
the picture flashed onto the screen, all of the arguments
and accusations that had been right on the tip of her
tongue died away.

There was her room. Only it wasn't her room. It was a
dream of her room, with vivid, deep blue walls. Walls that
were the color of her diving pool in Arizona, of the Agua
Azul waterfall she dove off of this summer, of the sparkling
ocean waters of Mexico that she'd come to love. It was a
mermaid color, a water goddess color, her color.

She heard Izzie calling that it was time to meet the bus
in town, so she shut off her laptop and picked up her bag,
still trying to take in what she'd just seen. Ted was right

about one thing. He had definitely surprised her this time.

The next afternoon, as she lay in the white sand on La Playa Condesa in Acapulco, all she could see was that *azul* color. It was in the ocean water, it was on the facade of the hotel they were staying at, it was everywhere. And each time she saw it, she felt a thrill of excitement. Soon, she'd be able to wake up and fall asleep with that deep blue surrounding her every day. It was almost enough to wash away some of the dread she felt about returning to Boston. Almost.

What she didn't want to think about was Ted. A heavy feeling in the pit of her stomach had started since she'd gotten his e-mail yesterday, and she couldn't shake it off. He had done something so nice for her, and she'd been giving him the silent treatment since his marriage to her mom.

For the first time in months, she was looking hard at herself, and she wasn't happy with what she was seeing. She didn't like the angry girl she'd become, or the way her voice had sounded all those times she'd yelled at her mom or Ted for no good reason. And she really didn't like the scared girl she'd become either—afraid to date, afraid to dive, afraid of getting hurt by her dad again, and most of all, afraid to like Ted. Afraid that he'd fill up her dad's place in her heart, or that he'd leave her and her mom heartbroken someday, too.

"What are you thinking about?" Aidan asked her, snapping her out of her thoughts.

"My family." Cat dug her toes into the sand, looking out at the water where Izzie, Sabrina, and the rest of the gang were bodysurfing in the waves. "When your dad remarried, were you ever scared that it would happen all over again? Another divorce, I mean."

Aidan nodded. "For a while, whenever my dad and my stepmom had a fight, even just a stupid one, I thought about it. But then I realized that if I stayed so freaked out all the time, I'd be miserable, even if they *never* got a divorce." He shrugged. "All you can do is deal the best you can when stuff happens that's out of your control."

Cat stared out at the ocean. "I'm starting to think that even if my mom and dad had stayed together, they might not have been happy. They have really different personalities. And my dad was always a little...removed...from our lives. It wasn't fair to my mom, or to me."

"And what about your mom and Ted?" Aidan asked. "Do they get along better?"

"Yeah, they seem to," she said. "So that's a good thing, at least. And my dad seems to be happy doing his own thing, too."

"So your parents figured out what they wanted, just like mine did," Aidan said. "What about you? If you had a choice, would you go back to the way things were two years ago, or stay in the now?"

"I don't know," Cat said. But in her heart, she thought that maybe she did know. She just wasn't ready to say it out loud yet.

Later that day, as Aidan led her into La Perla Restaurant, Cat tried one more time to get some info out of him.

"Won't you give me a little hint about what type of surprise this is?" she asked.

"Nope," Aidan said. "You'll just have to live with the suspense. Besides, you'll see for yourself soon enough."

Earlier, as they were packing up their beach bags to head back to the hotel, Aidan had told her to be ready by six P.M. for a special dinner date. It would just be the two of them, since Sebastian had given everyone a night of free time. Aidan wouldn't say a word about where they were going, but at six sharp he'd picked her up at her room, and they'd taken a twenty-minute walk up the steep hillside behind their hotel to La Perla, a restaurant overlooking the entire city and waterfront.

Now, as a waiter led them through the dining area, Cat teased Aidan, "Tell me this doesn't involve sacrificial virgins again."

Aidan shook his head. "No. But it does involve death-defying leaps of faith and flaming torches."

Cat laughed. "You know just how to keep a girl entertained."

The waiter took them out onto a huge candlelit patio,

and Cat gasped at the view before her. High, jagged cliffs, glowing a brilliant orange against the setting sun, dropped off steeply into a rough ocean inlet far below. The roaring waves crashing against the rocks below gave her chills.

"Wow," she said as they sat down at a table along the balcony. "It's beautiful."

"It's called La Quebrada," the waiter said. "The gorge. The pool of water at the bottom is only twelve feet wide by twenty-one feet deep." He handed them their menus. "Enjoy the show."

"Is this where the flaming torches come in?" Cat asked Aidan.

Aidan grinned. "Just keep your eyes on the cliffs."

They ordered their meal, and, as their food came, Cat kept checking the cliffs for a sign of activity. Fireworks maybe, or a laser light show. Soon, she saw a few people climbing to the top of the cliffs and a crowd gathering on a viewing platform below the restaurant.

It was just as their dessert arrived that Cat heard the cheers and clapping. She turned to see a man in a Speedo, silhouetted against the sinking sun, holding a flaming torch and standing at the very edge of the cliff.

"That's your surprise," Aidan said quietly. "In Spanish, they're called *las clavadistas*—cliff divers. They've been jumping here since the 1930s."

"My God," Cat gasped. "But that's a huge drop!"

"Forty-one meters," Aidan said. "I read up on it before

we came. He'll have to time his dive just right to miss the rocks below. And, he has to spin his body twenty feet away from the side of the cliff as he jumps to avoid hitting it."

Cat watched as the diver raised his arms and the flaming torch, lifted up on his toes for a split second, and then crouched and rocketed up into the air. He twisted out and away from the cliffside, streaming light from the torch he was holding as he moved. Arching gracefully like a soaring bird, he dove down, down, down into the water, and then shot straight into the sea. Cat shuddered at the loud smack as he hit the water, audible even from where she sat, hundreds of feet away.

To her relief, the diver bobbed back up to the surface to the cheers of the crowd. Several more divers took the plunge over the next half hour, and each time one leaped from the cliff, Cat imagined making the jump through the diver's eyes. It would be such an incredible rush to be in the air for that long, her muscles pulling her into the perfect dive as the wind whipped around her.

She was so involved in watching the diving show that she didn't even hear Aidan saying her name until he touched her hand.

"You want to be one of them, don't you?" he asked. "I can see it in that smile on your face. You love diving that much."

Cat thought about denying it, pretending not to care. But she didn't want to play that game anymore.

She finally nodded. "Yes, I do."

Aidan looked into her eyes. "Then whatever you do, don't give it up. Ever."

Cat looked back at La Quebrada. The crowds on the viewing platform had left, and the cliff had grown dark. The show was over.

"*¿Te gustan las clavadistas?*" their waiter asked when he returned with the bill.

"I loved it." Cat smiled. "But... do any women ever make the dive?"

The waiter nodded. "Just last year, a woman from the United States entered the world cliff-diving championship here. She was twenty-three years old."

"*Gracias,*" Cat said, her mind already spinning with possibilities. She hadn't even known there was a world diving championship. Could she even dream of doing such a thing? It would be the chance of a lifetime, that much she knew.

"It could be you out there, Cat," Aidan whispered. "Someday. But not if you quit."

For the first time since her move to Boston, she was out of excuses. She'd been so afraid that diving in Boston wouldn't match diving in Arizona. But the dive she'd made this summer at Agua Azul had thrilled her to the core. Diving would always be fantastic, no matter where she did it. In fact, she suddenly realized, there wasn't a reason in the world that was good enough for her to quit diving

when she loved it so much. Hopefully, if she was lucky, she still had time to do something about it.

That night, after Aidan kissed her good night and walked her to her room, Cat quickly logged on to her laptop, being careful not to wake Izzie. As her in-box popped onto the screen, she said a silent prayer that the e-mail was still there. She scanned through her Deleted Items folder, back to mail dated from the end of June, and her first few weeks in Mexico. There it was. The letter she'd been looking for from Coach Landon. Thank God she hadn't moved her deleted e-mails to her computer trash bin yet. She hit Reply and, with a pounding heart, wrote:

To: clandon@email.com
From: lilmermaid@email.com
Subject: Diving

Dear Coach Landon,
If the spots on the North Harbor Diving Club and varsity team are still open, I'd love to join. I hope it's not too late. Please let me know.
Thanks so much,
Caitlin Wilcox

The knock on her door came at one A.M.
"*¿Quién es?*" Izzie grumbled from her bed.

"I'll get it," Cat said, stumbling to the door. Through the peephole, she saw Sabrina, eyes red and tearing, shoulders shaking with sobs. Cat didn't ask any questions. Even through her sleepy haze, she'd already guessed what had happened. She just opened the door and took Sabrina by the hand, leading her into the room.

"I saw him tonight on the beach," Sabrina hiccuped when she'd calmed down enough to talk. "We went dancing with Rob and Amber and then to the beach with some university students we met at the club. I had a headache, so I decided to call it a night. Brian offered to walk me to the hotel, but I told him to stay. I got halfway here when I realized I'd left my sweater on the beach. I went back to get it, but Brian had disappeared from the group, so I went looking for him. And that's when I found him... with this girl from the club."

"A total ass," Cat said, handing Sabrina another tissue.

"*¡Exactamente!*" Izzie said.

"And he's so not earth-conscious either," Sabrina said. "Last week, I caught him using aerosol deodorant. And guess what his favorite food is?" She threw up her hands. "Veal marsala! That barbarian. He went on and on about 'global' community service, and the truth was he just wanted to bulk up his résumé for college." She sniffled. "I can't believe I fell so hard for some stupid guy."

"Hey," Cat said, pretending to be insulted. "Not all guys are stupid."

Sabrina gave a tired chuckle. "This from the girl who said she'd never date. Did you hear what you just said? You, my friend, have got it bad for Aidan."

Cat blushed. "Maybe I do." It was the first time she'd admitted it to herself, let alone out loud. But the more time she'd spent with Aidan, the more she felt like their dating could be the start of something that might last for a while. And that was a very good thing.

Sabrina yawned. "Do you think maybe I could crash on your floor tonight? Rachel's a great friend, but not such a great roommate. She snores."

Izzie and Cat both giggled at that, but Cat knew that the real reason Sabrina wanted to stay had nothing to do with Rachel. They'd gotten each other through so many tears back in Arizona with sleepovers, and now was no different.

"Sure," Cat said.

"Thanks." Sabrina nodded gratefully to Cat as Izzie switched off the light. Soon, a light fluttering sound came from Izzie's bed.

"Sabrina, you awake?" Cat whispered in the dark.

"Uh-huh."

"I forgot to tell you. Izzie snores, too."

Sabrina gave a hiccup of laughter as Cat giggled into her pillow.

"Cat?" Sabrina said, her voice quivering like she was crying again, or trying hard not to. "I'm so sorry for not believing you. I should have known you'd never lie to me."

Cat swallowed. She wanted to say that yes, Sabrina should've trusted her. But now wasn't the time for I-told-you-so's. Instead, she said simply, "Thanks."

"But you didn't like Brian, even from the beginning, did you?" Sabrina asked.

"No, I didn't," Cat said. "But it wasn't because I thought he was a jerk. Now I think he is, but at the beginning, I really didn't know him well enough to think that. I guess I was a little jealous. I wanted to spend the summer with you, hanging out like we used to in Scottsdale. I didn't want to share my best friend, especially after losing touch with Jason, Nikki, and everyone else in Arizona. And I was hurt that you didn't tell me about Brian before. In a way, I felt like *you* kind of lied to *me*."

"I wanted to tell you," Sabrina said. "But I was sort of mad at you, too. As soon as you moved to Boston, all you did was complain to me about how much you hated it and hated Ted. You stopped asking about what was going on with me."

"I did?" Cat said. She thought back on their nightly IM sessions, and all their e-mails and phone calls. Sure, she'd poured her own heart out, but how many times had she asked Sabrina about her life? She'd bugged Sabrina for news about the Scottsdale Diving Club and her friends, and Sabrina had sent sugarcoated IMs and e-mails full of school gossip. Cat had always assumed she'd be okay on her own. Until now, she'd never thought of what it was like

for Sabrina to lose her, either. "Maybe I did get stuck in pity-party mode for a while," she admitted.

"Yeah, you did," Sabrina said. "And I thought, well, if you weren't going to bother asking about my life, then I wasn't going to bother telling. I wanted you to feel bad, too. I guess we both acted like jerks."

"I'm sorry," Cat said.

"Me, too." Sabrina sighed. "You've always been the one who balanced me out, you know. Took me to the park or the pool for some downtime when I needed a break from the social scene at school. I missed that."

"And *you* somehow managed to convince me to go to school dances and parties when I felt like being antisocial, and *I* missed that." Cat smiled, remembering. "You probably could've done wonders for my social life in Boston."

"You would've done fine on your own if you'd let yourself," Sabrina said. "So we're okay now?" she asked tentatively. "We're not going to let anything get in the way of our friendship again, right?"

"Right." Cat smiled.

But even after they'd stopped talking, Cat couldn't sleep. She'd been through so much with Sabrina, and she'd always assumed they'd stay close, no matter where they lived, or what was happening in their lives. But this summer, they'd both changed. And after tonight, she was pretty sure that, even though their friendship was back on track, it would never be quite the same again.

Chapter Twelve

On the day of the school's grand opening, all of the host families came to see the final product and wait for the buses of orphans to begin arriving. The Canuls were one of the first families to arrive, carrying a large wrapped package with them.

"It's a folk-art piece from the gallery," Abril explained to Sebastian, "a gift for the children. It was painted by one of the Trique tribe who was an orphan himself."

Izzie and Cat hung it in a place of honor above the main doorway inside the school while Sebastian and Señor Sanchez set up a slide show in one of the classrooms. The

pictures followed the progress that had been made on the school over the last two months. In the first few, everyone looked dirty, tired, and sweaty in the middle of a field strewn with rocks and brush. Then there were pictures of the school under construction, the garden being planted, the playground being built, and, finally, pictures of everyone, a little tanned and a lot stronger, standing in front of the beautiful, finished school.

"Thanks to each and every one of you for putting your heart and soul into this project," Sebastian said, looking around the room with a proud smile. "Your efforts here won't be forgotten."

Just as the slide show finished, the orphanage buses pulled into the gravel parking lot, and children of all ages climbed excitedly out of them. As soon as the children saw the playground, the butterfly garden, and the classrooms with their books, toys, and colorful walls, it was all they could do not to trample one another to be first to try everything out.

Cat watched as a bunch of children surrounded Aidan and Pete, wanting to be spun around in a game of Superman that Aidan had started. Pete could pick up only the smallest kids, and even then, he tumbled melodramatically to the ground, letting the kids pile on top of him.

"Aidan and Pete look like they're having as much fun as the kids," Sabrina said as she walked over with Izzie.

Cat nodded. "Have you seen the Evil One Who Shall

Remain Unnamed?" she asked, using the new name for Brian that she'd come up with to keep Sabrina smiling.

Sabrina nodded. "He's over by the swing sets with Jimmy and Rob, gloating over his final grade."

They'd all gotten their finals back earlier that morning, and Cat had been thrilled to see her own A, feeling glad to be back on track with her grades.

"Well," she said, patting Sabrina's shoulder, "that just proves that good grades and good guys don't necessarily go together."

"He thinks he's a shoo-in for an Ivy League," Sabrina said.

"That may be," Cat said, "but even degrees from Stanford, Harvard, *and* Yale won't get him a girl as great as you again."

"I like the way you think," Sabrina said, giggling. She seemed to be doing a little better the last couple days, smiling and laughing more often. Cat had taken her for some last-minute souvenir shopping, and that had cheered her up, too. Cat bought herself some fun papier-mâché masks to hang on her newly painted bedroom walls, and some black-and-green pottery for her mom, something that Oaxaca was famous for. She'd even bought Ted a small book on Mexican history as a possible peace offering, but she couldn't decide whether or not she'd actually give it to him.

Sabrina, on the other hand, had bought some hand-

woven, earth-friendly clothes and decor for her room back home, proving she was well on the road to recovery. And for now, everyone, including Sabrina, was in a great mood seeing in the orphans' smiling faces how all their hard work on the school had paid off.

Cat watched one group of smaller children scramble up and down the slide in the playground, giggling all the way. "They love it," she said to Sabrina and Izzie. "It's amazing that they can be so happy, without any families of their own."

"Someday," Izzie said, "they could find parents. Some might be adopted in the United States. Some might never find real homes. But for now, they have families in one another."

"I guess there's all different kinds of families that work," Cat said. Suddenly, a wave of shame washed over her, and her eyes filled with tears.

"¿Que pasa?" Izzie asked, putting her hand on Cat's arm.

"I just realized how stupid I've been acting," Cat said. "I have a home—a great home. It's not exactly like I thought it would be, or where I wanted it to be, but still. These children don't have any parents, and I have three! And this whole time, I was wishing I didn't."

"You can still fix that," Izzie said with a smile.

Cat nodded, hoping that Izzie was right.

That night, Sebastian led the group and their host families back to La Casa de la Abuelita for a final dinner to celebrate the completion of the school and the end of the semester. Cat sat down with the Canuls, just as she had on her first night in Oaxaca, but this time, she didn't feel any of the awkwardness or nervousness she had back then. When she and Izzie headed to the buffet this time, she could easily identify almost every single food on the platters. Except one.

"Try one of these," Izzie said, stopping in front of the platter. "Another Mexican specialty."

"No way." Cat shook her head. "I'm not falling for that again. What are they?"

"Just tacos!" Izzie said, smiling innocently.

Cat looked around for Sebastian, and called him over. "What type of tacos are these?" she asked him.

"Tacos de sesos," he said.

"Brain tacos!" cried Cat as Izzie burst into laughter. "I knew it!" She elbowed Izzie playfully.

"They're made from cow brains," Sebastian said. "Actually quite tasty."

"I'll just trust you on that one," Cat said.

"See how much you've learned this semester?" Izzie said with a grin.

"And what about you?" Cat asked, following Izzie back to the table. "You would never have been introduced to the ingenious music of Tool or Anthrax if it weren't for me." Izzie had been listening to as many playlists on Cat's iPod as she could the last couple days, dreading having to part with it.

"Are you still going to burn those CDs for me when you get home?" Izzie asked.

"You'll get my entire *Gods of Metal* playlist on CD," Cat said. "Promise."

Abril and José smiled at the two girls as they sat down.

"Cat," Abril said, "you will always have a second home with us in Oaxaca."

"Thank you," Cat said. "And I hope you'll visit me in Boston someday, too, especially if Izzie comes to stay with us." She and Izzie had been talking just last night about Izzie's plan to come to the United States as a foreign exchange student next year. Cat was already plotting ways to convince her parents to let Izzie live with them in Boston for that semester.

She grinned at Izzie. "If you visit, I can introduce you to some American food specialties, like prairie oysters."

"*¡Deliciosa!*" Izzie said. "I love oysters."

But when Cat giggled at that remark, Izzie got defensive. "*¿Qué?* What? I do!"

"Good. We'll make sure you get some, then."

Cat gazed out on the *zócalo*, which was lit up with strings of white lights hanging from the rooftops of the cafés. A band was playing in the gazebo, and two salsa performers were dancing, trying to earn a few coins from tourists. One of them was a beautiful girl about Cat's age with thick hair twisted high on her head and large, catlike eyes. She walked around the café tables, inviting people to join her for a dance. As she came to the Helping Hands group, Brian walked over to her.

"If you're looking for a dance," Brian said, "I'm your man."

He gave her that same flirtatious grin Cat had seen him use on the girls at the beach and the salsa club in Mexico City. But *this* girl looked right past him. Her eyes focused only on her chosen potential dance partner: Pete.

"Check it out," Cat said, nudging Izzie. "She just blew off J.Crew boy for Petey."

"¡No lo creo!" Izzie said in disbelief as they watched.

"Con permiso," the girl said sweetly to Pete, who already had a look of total bliss on his face. *"¿Quieres bailar conmigo?"*

Pete bowed gallantly and took her hand. "I would love to dance with you." He grinned at Rachel and Aidan. "If you'll excuse me, my Spanish lady awaits."

"Blue Spanish eyes," he sang as he followed the dancer out into the square. "Prettiest eyes in all of Mexico."

"I don't believe it." Cat laughed.

"Quien con la esperanza vive, alegre muere." Izzie smiled. "He who lives with hope, dies a happy man."

Watching Pete's delirious smile as he danced, Cat laughed. "He *does* look like he's in heaven. And all this time, I thought he was just delusional."

"No," said Izzie. "But it *is* a good thing I taught him how to salsa. If he's going to be a Don Juan, he better have some rhythm."

Soon, Abril and José joined in the dance, and Aidan took a few turns with Cat, Izzie, Sabrina, and Rachel. Only Brian stayed sitting moodily at the café with his host family, and Cat was secretly glad to see him just the tiniest bit miserable. It was probably a little snarky, but hey, the guy had broken her best friend's heart without so much as an "I'm sorry." If his only comeuppance was getting dissed for Pete, he should consider himself lucky. Aidan and Pete had made a few joking offers to kick his butt, but Cat had said drily, "Violence is not the answer."

"That's a relief," Pete had said. "The guy outweighs me by a hundred pounds. My short but sexy life was flashing before my eyes."

As Cat danced the last salsa of the night with Aidan, she looked around at all her new friends. Izzie and José were dancing now, Abril had convinced Sebastian to join her, and Rachel and Sabrina were dancing together, laughing away.

She'd started this semester thinking only about how much she wanted to get back to Arizona to be with all of her old friends, and in just a couple months, she'd made new friends from all over the United States and Central America. Funny how the summer she'd thought everything was falling apart became the summer that everything had come together so perfectly.

After she'd enjoyed a few hours of visiting with Abril, José, and Izzie, and packed her bags for her flight home the next morning, Cat checked her e-mail one last time. She'd been checking it every day, several times a day, since she had e-mailed Coach Landon, and finally, tonight, there was an e-mail reply from him. "I'm delighted to hear that you've changed your mind," he wrote. "And of course, we'd love to have you on the teams. I'll see you at the first practice on Monday."

Cat smiled as she logged off. Her heart was already racing with excitement at the thought of diving on the three-meter board at the North Harbor Diving Club. She was dying to share the news with someone, and she knew the perfect person to tell. She took a seat in the Canuls' courtyard under the starlit sky and dialed home. Her heart flopped when Ted picked up the phone.

"Hi, Ted," she started awkwardly. "It's Caitlin. I mean, Cat. It's Cat."

"Hi, Cat," he said. "Your mom's at the grocery store. I can tell her you called—"

"Actually," she said, rushing through her words, "I, um, called to talk to you."

"Oh?"

Cat smiled a little. Ted wasn't very good at hiding the surprise in his voice, but she couldn't really blame him. She would've been surprised, too, if she had a stepdaughter who suddenly developed an uncanny ability to speak to her.

"I wanted to say"—she took a deep breath—"thanks. For painting my bedroom. I like it. No...I love it. I can't wait to see it."

Several seconds passed painfully before Ted spoke.

"I'm glad to hear that," he said. "I was worried it might be the wrong shade."

"It's perfect," Cat said. "And...I also wanted to tell you that I e-mailed Coach Landon, and I'm joining the diving club and the varsity team."

Ted cleared his throat, and Cat could've sworn she could actually hear him smiling on the other end of the line. "That's great news," he said. "Your mom will be very pleased when she finds out. And I'm pleased." He paused. "I'm proud of you, Cat."

Cat blushed in the darkness, and was very grateful no one was around to see it. "Thanks," she said. "And one more thing, Ted. Maybe we could go out for doughnuts sometime after I get home? I can show you how to eat them with your fingers without a mess, and without the fork and knife."

His deep belly chuckle burst into the phone, making Cat giggle. "I'd like that," he said. "I'd like that very much."

After Cat hung up, she leaned back, gazing up at the stars. Ted had been trying to befriend her for so long, and for so long she'd been pushing him away. Now, for the first time, she was going to give him the benefit of the doubt. And while she was at it, she'd give Aidan's Best of Boston list a try. And maybe even make a real effort to meet some of the kids at North Harbor High, too. It was time to give Ted, her *azul* bedroom, and her life in Boston a chance.

The next morning, Cat fought back a few tears as she hugged the Canuls good-bye before boarding the bus to the Oaxaca airport.

"*Aquí está algo pequeño para ti.* This is something small for you," Izzie said, handing Cat a package. "From all of us."

Cat unwrapped it to reveal a book-sized painting of a cliff diver leaping gracefully into the waters of Acapulco.

"Aidan saw it when he came by to pick up some art for his parents. He told us you might like it," Abril said. "Next time you visit Mexico, maybe we'll see you make this dive?"

"Maybe," Cat said, smiling. "Thank you all so much."

She boarded the bus and waved at the Canuls until the bus rounded the corner of the *zócalo*. Then she stared down at the painting of the diver in her hands. She'd hang it up over her bed as soon as she got home.

Once they arrived at the airport, Sabrina's flight was announced first, and Aidan waited patiently while Cat said good-bye.

"I'll e-mail you," Sabrina said.

"You better." Cat smiled. "I want to hear all about your latest crush." At Sabrina's doubtful look, she added, "I know there'll be one."

"We'll see. I'm taking a break from guys for a while," Sabrina said. "It'll be nice to make my own plans and do my own things for a change. But I want to hear how the diving goes." Then she leaned closer to whisper out of Aidan's earshot, "And, of course, the latest details on your now-totally-official boyfriend."

"You'll be the first to know." Cat laughed.

"Do you think you'll still come back to Arizona U for college?" Sabrina asked.

Cat hesitated. Two months ago, she would've said yes without a doubt, but now she wasn't so certain. "I don't know. It all depends on this next year. I bet there are some great bilingual study programs in New England, too. I might look into a few of those. Anything could happen, and I want to keep my options open."

"Well," Sabrina said. "Maybe we both got something we needed this summer. You're a little more hopeful about dating, and I'm a little more cynical about it." She shrugged. "Given my track record with guys, that might not be such a bad thing."

She smiled. "We'll stay in touch, no matter what."

"I'll be back in Scottsdale to see my dad at Christmas," Cat said. "And of course we'll keep in touch 'til then." But as they hugged one more time, it was hard for Cat to fight back tears. Even though they were making all these promises like they had so many times before, for the first time it felt like they might be saying good-bye to a part of their friendship, too. Both of them had changed so much over the summer, and Cat felt like she might have outgrown some of her need to be in constant touch with Sabrina. It was time for her to make some new friends in Boston. Sabrina would always be there for her, but she didn't need to be the only one Cat relied on anymore.

After Sabrina disappeared through her gate, Cat walked to hers with Aidan.

"Are you dreading going back home?" he asked.

Cat thought about that for a minute before answering. "I thought I would be. But the funny thing is, I'm not. At least not like I was at the beginning of the semester."

Aidan grinned. "Good. Because, you know, I can't be hanging out with a downer in New York. It'd cramp my style."

"And who says we'll be hanging out?" Cat teased. "You haven't asked me to yet, so how do you know I want to?"

Aidan leaned toward her. "Because," he said with a smile, "you find me irresistible. And if I ask you to come visit me in Manhattan, you'll say, 'Yes, Aidan, I'd love to.' "

"On one condition," Cat said, smiling.

"What's that?"

"That you agree to visit me in Boston, too."

Aidan seemed to be deep in thought. Finally, he said, "One question: You're not going to drag me to any Red Sox games, are you? Because that's where I draw the line."

"I swear I won't." Cat laughed.

"Then it's a done deal. So, do you want to come visit me in Manhattan?"

Cat grinned. "I'd love to."

Aidan pulled out his sketchbook and carefully tore out the Best of Boston list. "Hang on to this, and every time I come up to see you, we'll do something on it."

Cat skimmed the list. "There are over twenty things here."

"I added some yesterday. I needed a few more excuses to visit you." He smiled. "So, what's your final verdict after this summer? Are you happy?"

The question took Cat by surprise. She'd spent so much of the last year trying to prove how unhappy she was. This summer had been her plan to make herself happy, but none of it had gone the way she'd imagined. Not even close. Now, when she looked back on all the things she'd seen and done, and the new friends (and maybe even boyfriend?) she'd met, her summer, with all its pitfalls, seemed better than she'd ever expected. Making new friends had been worth the effort, even if they weren't the same as her old ones. She'd have to make more in Boston, too.

"Yes," she said with a smile. "I am happy."

And she was. If she could survive the summer in a whole new country, she could certainly survive the rest of the year in a new state, and have a great time doing it.